DRAG WARS

Fangula vs Pridezilla

Robert A. Karl

Published by Robert A. Karl
First Edition June 2024
ISBN: 979-8-9879126-6-9 (Paperback)
ISBN: 979-8-9879126-7-6 (Ebook)

The domain fangula.com is registered to the author, Robert A. Karl. All Rights Reserved.

This book is entirely the author's creation. AI was not used in any way, and the use of the contents of this book for AI machine learning is expressly forbidden.

Cover Design: Krishna (fiverr.com/nirkri)

Images licensed through Shutterstock.

Acknowledgments

I want to thank the following people for their support during the process of bringing this book to life.

Thank you, **Jorge Carrasquillo**, for your words of encouragement and advice.

Also, thanks to **Rayceen Pendarvis**, for opening doors and introducing me to members of the drag community.

My special thanks go to the following Drag Queens, for being so kind and sharing information about their drag experiences with me. I am forever in your debt.

Robusta Capp

Tara Hoot

Shi-Queeta-Lee "Diva of TOWN"

Dedication

Welcome

WELCOME TO DRAG WARS

I don't appear in drag to hide myself from the world. The truth is, I use the art of drag to show the world who I truly am.

~Fangula, on www.fangula.com

Drag isn't what I do. Drag is who I am.

~ Pridezilla

Contents

CASA DE FUEGO

My fluttering fan brings no relief from the intense tropical heat generated by the dancing bodies of a thousand people swarming in the club. That's how it is on Friday night at Club Fuego, the night when we take over. The Queers, the Queens, the Fashionistas, even the Bizarros. Starved for attention, thirsty for love, even for a moment. This isn't a jeans and tee shirt crowd. People here want to stand out. And who can blame them? When society treats you as invisible, the desire to be seen, to be admired, to be noticed, is felt intensely.

A few expert snaps of the fan, adorned with butterflies, one of the most beautiful in my collection, command the attention of the dancers surrounding me. Pointing towards the balcony, I direct my entourage to our destination.

The guys I refer to as my entourage are actually just a small group of friends. One day, I hope to have a real entourage, selected by me personally from a huge group of my fans. And I want to give them a nickname, like Gaga has her Little Monsters and Beyoncé has her BeyHive. I've considered calling them "The Littles," but I haven't shared that with anyone yet. Or, maybe I'll call them "The Cruzers," since my last name is Cruz.

There's no rush to decide at this moment. However, I think it's best to be prepared for these small details. Fame can spring very quickly, you know.

Walking towards the bar, my eyes glued to the man working there, I'm momentarily distracted by the glaring stares of the Snark Sharks, led by their villainous Queens, Ru-Barb and Nepharious. Just as I'm passing close by, I snap my fan directly at Ru-Barb. Not once, but twice. That could be interpreted as a direct challenge.

Damn, now why in the fuck did I do that? Those Queens might come in handy one day, if I can get close enough to them to learn what they like and most importantly, what they don't like about particular acts. It isn't my intention to make enemies of them. I have enough of those already.

Just like the Great Whites rule the seas as apex predators, the Snark Sharks do their best to rule the club. Their level of success is debatable. Ru-Barb and Nepharious form the core of the group, but they are often joined by others — queens who are mostly older, somewhat jaded, and definitely sharp-tongued. They have developed the ability to find every flaw in each performance and love to gossip mercilessly about the Queens on the stage.

Why do this? That's the game, part of drag culture.

The Snark Sharks are the Philly version of "Spillin' the Tea" or "The Pit Stop," which feature former *Drag Race* contestants giving their often-hilarious commentaries about the show created by RuPaul and loved by millions.

Many times, it's done all in good fun, but let's face it, some of those comments come equipped with barbed arrows. Personally, I think it helps Queens develop the toughness that's required to confront the world with our Drag Fierceness. If you can't take it from our own kind, how in the hell will you survive the comments thrown at you by your sworn enemies?

Too easily distracted by the man behind the bar, the handsome Eliud, and starting to feel the drinks hitting me hard, I missed the first act. The Snark Sharks, however, could be heard clear across the room as they offered their thoughts.

"She did get her name right, at least," crows Ru-Barb. "Mama Casa fits, 'cause she's big as a fuckin' house, but that's about the only thing I liked. My god, that outfit!"

"Where in the fuck did she ever find that horrid fabric? It looks like something from an Amish quilting bee," sniffs Nepharious, as she gulps her vodka spritz. Heavy on the vodka and very, very light on the seltzer, just as she likes it.

"If I had to look at it for even a moment longer, I was worried I'd lose the sight in my other eye," laments Miss Dee Eyed, who had actually lost an eye in the war in Afghanistan. "Imagine if I had to wear two eye patches!"

"Lemme get an order in on DoorDash. One extra-large ham sandwich for Mama Casa!" Nepharious says, as the Sharks double over in laughter.

"No gurl, not that! Do not even go there!" Miss Dee Eyed screams while Ru-Barb places her hands around her throat, making gagging noises.

"All right, I gotta do this," Ru-Barb states firmly, standing to get the attention of the crowd surrounding the stage. "Ladies, I'm throwing out the Blue Bra of Shame for that wretched performance. And with that, Ru-Barb pulls a blue bra out of her bag with the word 'SHAME' written across it in red marker, and swings it over her head before tossing it onto the stage.

Sitting close to the Sharks, I hang onto every word.

"Why you listenin' to them oldies?" my bestie, Whitey, asks. You wanna get a reputation like theirs? Bitter, old, gossipy queens?"

"Well, at least then I'd have a rep," I reply, "instead of sittin' up here as a spectator all the time. I wanna be in the show, not watchin' the goddamn thing."

And then the show continues as Divinity Thee Goddess is being introduced. My former friend is about to perform, but since we're now fighting over the same man, well, my feelings have changed. Before she even starts, the liquid courage from my 4th Appletini leads me to blurt out, "Your culo's been invaded so often there's room for the entire Russian Army up in there!"

My high-pitched voice pierces through the noise, the foggy effects and the general chaos of the club, as Divinity casts a glance skyward, confirming what she already knew. That I was the perpetrator. I pretend not to care that even our MC, Sir Janus, turns his face into a disapproving frown.

The Master of Ceremonies for this evening, Sir Janus, aka El Rey, never tolerates outright rudeness. Jeering at a poor performance, no

4

problem. Screaming ridiculous insults, especially from someone as drunk as I clearly was—that's a hard No. And Janus wants to be in control. Correct that, Janus is in control.

"You, up on the balcony, I'm 'bout ready to kick your ass out until you learn how to show a little respect!"

At that word, everybody in the audience joins in, shouting, "R - E - S- P - E - C - T. That's Respect!"

Even I join in, though I'm the one being reprimanded by the King on the stage. Better to blend in right now than show my ass even more and get kicked out.

After all, this is my second home. Fuego, the one club in the 'hood that has "Gay Night" every Friday night, with occasional pop-up nights for special occasions.

Though it's Friday, it's still a special celebration in honor of the host's 30th birthday. The Queens are puttin' on a show, each trying to impress, not only the crowd, but also trying to earn an invitation to the next event by impressing King Janus.

Dramatically taking the stage, Divinity momentarily ignores the audience, instead focusing her steely glare directly at me. Using both hands, giving me the universal sign of disrespect with her professionally polished middle fingers pointing at me, she mouths the words, "Fuck off, Nadie!"

That's what they call me. Nadie. Nobody. And that is who I am. At least for now, because I still haven't figured out my drag name. I desperately want to be a performer, but every Drag Queen needs a name, and until I figure this out, I'll remain Nadie.

After that, I refuse to even watch her performance. Oh, I hear the crowd cheering for her. And I know the tips are flying in her direction.

But this passive-aggressive Queen chooses to be as aggressively passive as possible, by having my quiet tantrum at the bar, furious at Divinity because of the attention she's getting. Okay, so color me jealous. That's really ain't nothing new for me.

Besides my jealousy at her performance, there is one other little thing. Both of us are after the same man. That's why I'm sitting where I can stare at the man behind the bar rather than watching the show. This bartender, Eliud, the one all the Queens are after, is gonna be my man, at least for tonight. And after he gets a taste of this bussy, well, I think he's gonna be hooked.

As the show continues, the MC King Janus strides from stage right to stage left, marching to an unheard drumbeat. He easily commands both the stage and the assembled crowd, including not only Queers, but also the neighborhood freaks, drunks, and troublemakers with ease. Club Casa de Fuego attracts all sorts of folks, especially on Drag Nights.

Tonight's drag outfit is military, done to perfection. All 6 feet of Janus, in this exact outfit, could stride onto any Marine base without being questioned. Besides passing as a Marine, no one on a military base would ever suspect that Sir Janus's birth certificate had identified him as a female.

I'm not even sure that everyone in the club knows Janus's story. He is the undisputed King of the Cabaret, the Master of Ceremonies, emphasis on Master. He's in command, no doubt. It's questionable how many here recognize that he's a trans man. Many in the audience assume that he's a gay guy.

After Divinity's performance, he raises his hand to bring the crowd to silence, his voice used as a weapon to control the at-times unruly crowd. He's spent hours practicing that voice, vowing that he'll not only look as masculine as possible, but sound the part as well.

I, on the other hand, use my sweet, sultry voice to issue my own command to the only person in the club I truly cared about.

"Refill, Whitey," I whisper, limply dangling my empty glass in front of him.

"No, Donnie. You had too much already."

Whitey is used to my erratic behavior, so it doesn't surprise him when I weakly fling my martini glass at the wall, not even denting the cheap plastic, which tumbles silently to the floor.

"Fine!" I say, brushing past him, waving him off, dismissing my best friend. "I'll get it myself."

Trying to steady myself as I head for the bar, where the hot, handsome Latino bartender is sure to give me anything I want, I vaguely hear Janus introducing the next act.

"Ladies, ladies, and others, please welcome to the stage, the lovely, dynamic Miss Wilma Tsetse Fly!"

Whitey bends over with laughter. "You hear that name, Donnie? That's a drag name supreme. Wilma Tsetse Fly! Yeah, I wanna see if her teeties gonna fly! Yeah!"

The music starts as Wilma takes to the stage, but I only catch a small part of her act. I'm too busy lusting after that fine Puerto Rican man behind the bar to pay attention to anything or anyone else.

Whitey, however, enjoys every moment of the show. Wilma is decked out, looking beyond extra, in her self-made costume with five pairs of detachable, stacked "breasts." Naturally, the biggest set, covering all the others, is positively humongous.

Sitting on a stool in front of a mirror on stage, her act consists of her serenading herself with the song "Beautiful," by Christina Aguilera. Working through the lyrics, she keeps removing her boobs, making her chest grow progressively smaller, questioning society's obsession with larger breasts being equated with greater beauty. Once Wilma removes the final set of boobs, she lowers the straps of her dress, revealing her bare chest, then removes her earrings and finally, her wig. Turning to the audience, she looks sad, asking the audience not to bring her down. "Because after all, we are beautiful," she whispers into the mike.

The audience loves the show, and Wilma has tips galore to collect as she's showered with appreciative cheers.

The Snark Sharks aren't impressed...or kind.

"Anybody singin' that song oughta at least look like Miss Christina, don't ya think? The resemblance here ain't exactly amazing," blurts Ru-Barb.

Miss Dee Eyed: "Is a tsetse fly kind of like a mosquito? 'Cause her voice sounded like one was buzzing around on the stage."

Ru-Barb: "Haven't we seen this same act over and over?"

Miss Dee Eyed: "I don't know, doll. Lemme check my index cards. You know I got an eye for the details."

Ru-Barb: "An eye? Did you really say you got an eye?"

Everybody laughs as Miss Dee takes it in stride. She accepts that she lost an eye, never trying to hide the fact. She often wears a rainbow-colored patch as an accessory, proud of her gayness and of her sacrifice for the country.

Nepharious: "Back to Wilma, I was hoping she'd come out swinging a club. You know, like on *The Flintstones*. Her skin looks like she'd be well-acquainted with that family from Bedrock. All those wrinkles! She never heard of moisturizer?"

Miss Dee Eyed: "And I wasn't sure if her makeup was on wrong or if her rosacea was actin' up."

Nepharious: "Ru, what did you write on the bill before you threw it on the stage?"

Ru-Barb: "I only tipped her one dollar and I wrote, 'Get a pedi!' I mean, with those open-toed shoes, everyone can see those jagged toenails. Has she no shame?"

They could carry on and on, seemingly without regard for the time and effort each performer puts into preparing their acts.

Whitey, however, loved the show and enjoyed telling me the next day all about Wilma's "tsetses," and how he was moved by the lyrics and the presentation.

THREE AMIGAS

Whitey comes over to my apartment, a third-floor walkup on "G" Street, in the Kensington section of my hometown, Philadelphia. I'm still in bed, with my Rican man, *mi caco*, when he knocks on the door around noon. Elie quickly gets up, dressed, and heads out the door, choosing not to join us for breakfast. Not even a coffee.

"Call me later, Eliud," I tell him, as he brushes by Whitey at the front door, while lightly touching my cheek, sending a tingle up my spine. I know my type, and Elie is it. Whitey, however, has his doubts.

What makes me happy this morning is that Eliud came to my place last night, so I'm one up on my rival, Divinity. We were friends, but when it comes to getting a man, well, what's more important? A friendship, or getting the man I want? Friendships are a dime a dozen, right?

My little brother, Carlito, emerges from his bedroom, heading straight for the kitchen.

"We gonna watch them makeup videos on YouTube today? You know we gotta practice in case you ever come up with a decent name and can get up on that stage."

He winks at Whitey, knowing it'll get under my skin that I still haven't decided on my drag name.

The delectable scent of the frying bacon and *huevos* fills our small kitchenette, as Carlito hums a Spanish tune, swaying his hips to the beat of the music coming from his phone, perched on the top of the fridge.

"Yeah, yeah, YouTube is the plan for today. We don't want them queens makin' those vids to be wastin' their time and talents."

Whitey has been my best friend ever since we were both in the same 5th Grade class at Roberto Clemente Middle School. Of course, Whitey isn't his real name. But as the only Caucasian boy in the entire 5th Grade at Clemente, he stuck out like an albino in a sea of rainbow trout.

I still remember our homeroom teacher, Ms. Castillo, calling out his name. "Franklin Mayflower! Franklin Mayflower!"

I had never heard a name like that, so I looked around and saw him. Snickering, I nudged the boy next to me and said, "How fuckin' white do you gotta be to get a name like Franklin Mayflower?"

Then, I blurted out for the whole class to hear, "Hey Whitey, what the hell did you do to get sent here? Violate your parole?"

"Yeah, they caught me in a violation...violatin' your Mama!" he snapped back, earning the instant respect of everyone in the class except the teacher, Ms. Castillo, who showed her disapproval, referring both of us to the Principal's office. And on the first day of school!

From that point forward, everyone called him Whitey. Except the teachers, of course. To them, he was always "Franklin."

Not that I had room to talk. My Mami, apparently expecting me to take on the hyper-masculine features and attitudes of my machismo father, had named me "Adonis."

Adonis Manlee Cruz, no less. Talk about a name not matching the flower. Better I had been named Rosa Flores. But that, of course, was my secret, at least in the 5th Grade—or so I told myself. The truth is, I started acting in my feminine ways long before I got to Clemente Middle School.

Teachers have a funny thing about names. They seem to prefer calling every student by their given first name, whether the student prefers that or not. Maybe they think they're being respectful, but I didn't see it that way. At least, that's how I felt back at Clemente.

It was always, "Adonis, stop talking in class!" or "Adonis, pay attention!" or "Adonis, keep your eyes on your own paper!"

Adonis, Adonis, Adonis. I hated it, because it made the other kids laugh at me, tease me, mock me. They would say things like, "Adonis sucks dick!" or "Adonis the pussy," or "Adonis looks like a girl."

It was useless to argue, especially about my looks. I did look like a girl. A beautiful girl. And when I acted out, I did it like a girl. I admit it now. I accept it now. Back then, I had no idea why I acted the way I did.

But school was a long time ago. I just barely graduated 8th Grade. I wasn't willing to continue failing in the eyes of teachers and being subjected to the opinions of the "smarties," especially at a place like Kensington High School, the next stop after Clemente. That place was rough, and it wasn't lost on me that I'd be a constant target. So, I left before anyone even had the chance to bully me into submission. The last day of 8th Grade was my final day of formal schooling.

I never would have made it through middle school if it wasn't for Whitey, who acted as my protector. But even he couldn't protect me from the worst tormentors, some of the teachers there. Mr. Davidson, the Science teacher, referred to me as "The Little Diva" in front of the entire class.

"Do you know the answer, my little chiquita?" he'd ask, as the rest of the class snickered. Or, he'd say, "Would the little diva like to try to answer the question?" Later, in the lunch room, I'd be tormented by every boy, pulling my hair or slapping me as they walked by, telling me that I was their "chiquita," their "little girl."

At Clemente Middle, if a boy liked a girl, the rest of the boys would dare him to touch her butt. It's a ritual. But in my case, boys would dare other boys to touch my butt. Some took the dare. Others declined. I always wondered why. Did the boys who took the dare want something from me? Did they want my butt? Oh, the games boys play!

Now, I make enough money as a waiter at Rico, one of the most popular Latino restaurants in Philly, to rent this apartment and take care of my little brother. And no, I'm not going to let him drop out, even though I already see the signs that he wants to give up, too.

Not that I've given up on life. Far from it. I only gave up the academic, scholarly life. That isn't for me. But I do have dreams. Big dreams. Mostly, they involve being on the stage, as a Queen. I want to be the Queeniest Queen that ever queened.

As Carlito serves the breakfast plates, Whitey suggests a change in plans. "Instead of sittin' in and studyin' makeup, how about we head downtown and hit up the fabric stores?"

We have an ongoing argument about which comes first while designing a drag look—the makeup or the costume. I'm not that good at sewing, so I try to argue that the makeup should be decided first, and then the costume should complement that design.

"You're fuckin' cray cray," Whitey would argue. "It's the fabric and everything else that goes into the costume that costs the most and takes the most time. So, it only makes sense to have the makeup ideas come later on in the process. Isn't that right, Lito?"

We already know that Carlito agrees with Whitey. And I know it makes sense. But, I like to be obstinate sometimes, even though I might (at least in this instance) be wrong.

The decision is made. Fabric Row is our destination for the day. Fourth Street, just below Bainbridge, has a cluster of stores specializing in fabrics. We're headed to Fabrizio's Fabrics.

"Off to Mood!" I shout, while we finish eating, making a reference to the fabric store used by the designers on *Project Runway*. But unlike the show, we aren't given a budget by a famous fashion designer. And we aren't on a tight timeline, just to create a little drama for a TV audience.

We're three gay guys on a mission to find fabulous fabrics within our budget to be used to create a costume fit for a Queen.

On a side note, yes, Carlito, who's actually my half-brother, is definitely gay. But he's only 14 years old. I'm not sure he's figured it out for himself, but my gaydar goes off loud and clear in his presence.

And I do believe he's still a virgin. That's what I hope, anyway. But if he isn't...well, who am I to lecture anyone about losing their virginity at an early age?

Sir Janus has his life much more in order than mine. But that's to be expected, since he just turned 30 and has already made some major life decisions. He rules the stage at Fuego on Friday nights, but that's only a small part of his life.

After graduating from the Fashion Institute of Technology, he moved from New York to Philly, gradually transitioning from being perceived as a female to living full-time as a male. This doesn't happen overnight, but Janus was adamant about attaining his goals. His transition was one goal. Owning his own fashion line is another.

At this point in time, he owns one of the stores on Fabric Row, living in the apartment on the second floor with his wife and young daughter, in the heart of Queen Village. His wife, Genesis, is a recent graduate of the Beasley School of Law at Temple University, and she just started a position with Fernandez and Associates, a small law firm on Chestnut Street.

The three of us are often viewed with suspicion when we go into Center City Philly, especially when we travel together.

After we hop off the El at 5th and Market Streets, we decide to walk the rest of the way to Fabric Row. Ignoring all the historical buildings in the area is easy for us. Crowded with tourists, there's nothing of interest to us there. After all, we're on a treasure hunt.

Crossing through Independence Mall, we casually stroll down 4th Street, not in any particular hurry. Passing through a residential area, the streets grow quiet. No loud groups of tourists, chattering about whatever occupies their minds at the moment.

I feel alone with my thoughts.

And I'm thinking about names.

Drag names.

But I'm not feeling inspired—certainly not by these colonial-style townhomes, not by the historical significance of this neighborhood. Only the Richie Riches live here. I imagine them in their carefree lives of luxury, never having to worry about surviving—like I do.

Carlito and Whitey are having an animated conversation that had escaped me while I was daydreaming.

"I watched *Barbie* again last night and Ken is so obviously gay! G-A-Y, gay, gay, gay! He was flutterin' like a *mariposa*!" Whitey shouts, trying to make his point by being loud about it.

"But he loved Barbie. That's the very definition of bein' a straight boi. C'mon man, Ken wanted some of that good female lovin'! You saw that part, right?" counters Carlito.

It's at that point that I decide to jump into the conversation.

"How the hell can Ken be gay? He ain't even got no dick. They even said it right there in the movie. What's he gonna do with the other Kens, huh? They gonna bump their plastic together?"

"Well if he can't be gay, how can he be straight?" Whitey asks, barely getting the words out through his laughter. "If he ain't got the dick, Barbie ain't got no place for him to put it anyways! Amirite?"

"They just dolls, remember? Why we even discussin' this when we got ourselves a real doll right here and we gotta plan how to dress her up?"

Of course, Whitey is referring to me. The baby doll. Is that who I want to be? A doll to be dressed up by my friends? Or something more?

As we pass a barbershop with a large front window, I stop, wrapping my arms around my two best friends.

"Look at us," I say, motioning toward our reflections. "What do you see?"

"The Three Amigas?" Whitey answers, trying to be cute.

I could've slapped him. I'm feeling serious, but I also understand the urge to joke about everything.

"No, stop. Take a minute and think. Take a good look at us. What do you see? Who are we, really?"

Pondering our reflections for a few seconds, we become strangely silent. Not usually serious about things, our banter is normally non-stop.

What I see in the glass are three young men, with certain similarities, but each unique.

Physically, we have much in common. Our heights range from 5'6" to 5'7", not much of a spread. All three of us are slim and trim, though my crop top reveals a tight waist that lacks abs, but with the cutest little belly button you ever did see.

Whitey and Carlito are wearing graphic tees, hiding their waists, but I already know that Whitey's abs are impressive while Carlito, the youngest of the group, could use a few sit-ups to tighten himself up. He isn't heavy, but he doesn't make any effort to work on his body. I hope he doesn't end up taking after his father, who was heavyset. Right now, his body is soft, so I poke him in the belly as we watch our reflections and laugh.

Carlito and I have the same Latina mother, but my father was white and his father was Black. Neither of the men had stayed with our mom, and now, none of us were living with her. But the result is that Lito's skin is several shades darker than mine. Whitey, as the name suggests, is pale in comparison to both of us. The reflections of our faces show the hopes of young, handsome men, who perhaps don't quite yet know what life has to offer us.

Well, perhaps the word "handsome" doesn't describe each of us. Carlito and Whitey, yes. But me, I'm the "pretty" one. More feminine than the other two combined.

I wonder if that's a blessing or a curse, but there's no denying that my brilliant green eyes attract a lot of attention. I smile at myself in the reflection. I like what I see. My flamboyant mannerisms are part of what makes me stand out. And though I know there are times when that can put me in danger, I refuse to change to suit what other people want. These streets can be mean, so it's always good to have a couple of my *amigos* around.

"Gurl, I ain't know what the hell you want us to see, but I'm agreein' with Whitey. I still see the Three Amigas!" Carlito laughs, dragging us past the window, heading for our destination.

THE NAME GAME

As we near the shop, I stop to quickly fix my blonde hair, which is growing long and has been getting a bit tangled in the breeze. Combing it out, I decide to fix my face, applying a fresh bit of blush and adding more lipstick. Carlito looks a little annoyed, as he had done my makeup before we left the apartment, but I ignore his look.

Located just a few doors below Bainbridge Street on 4th stood Fabrizio's Fabrics, our favorite shop for costume materials. Our "MOOD," as it were.

The owner buzzes us in, the locked door being a holdover from the days of the COVID pandemic, when the city was on lockdown for months that seemed endless.

"Welcome, hunties!" he beams at us. "Looking a little on the hungover side today, amirite?"

"Especially you, my dear," he continues, walking towards me and cupping my chin in his hand. "You naughty little thing. I thought

I taught you how to show respect!" With that, he double-snaps his fingers in my face.

Although I know I was wrong last night, I wasn't planning on being read forever about it, so I stand my ground.

"Miss Divinity Thee Goddess had it coming. Maybe you don't know the whole story, Fabrizio."

My statement was met with silence, as King Janus thought about what I had just said.

"Children, go about your business, assuming you know what you're looking for. I want to speak to Miss Thing here privately."

"Go, minions!" I command in my best Christian Siriano voice. "You have 30 minutes to shop!"

At least that brought a smile to Janus's face. "Oh, a *Project Runway* fan, I see. Very funny! Is that what you want to be when you grow up? Another Christian Siriano?

"No, I don't want to be him. I want him to design a look for me. Maybe for my first appearance at the Met Gala!"

"I like your style. Dream big!" Janus says.

Lito and Whitey scurry off to find the red and black fabrics I want for my next costume. I turn to face the King, wondering what I'd done to upset him.

"Let's talk about stories, child. It's true, I don't know your full story, and I'd like to know more. But clearly, you don't know my story, either, or you'd never have called me Fabrizio."

"But...but the name outside on the sign"...I stammer.

"Darlin', do you know that I'm a trans man? I only ask because not everyone realizes it," Janus says.

"Yeah, I know. At least, that's what I had heard. People do talk, ya know."

"Yes, they most certainly do," Janus agrees. "So, let me try to follow your train of thought. You know I'm trans, and I'm a man, and my name is Janus, right?"

"Yes, that's right," I reply.

"Then you do realize that I was born and raised as a female...and I transitioned...and yet somehow you think I was named Fabrizio at birth? Does that make any sense to you?"

"Well, now that you mention it..."

"And besides the obvious stupidity of that thought process, you then thought it was appropriate to dead-name me here in my shop, in front of my face?"

"Dead-name you...I would never!" I protest.

"Honey, that's exactly what you did, which is why I want to clear the air right here and now."

As I realize just how wrong I was, embarrassment consumes me. What a stupid mistake to make!

"Let's press the reset button and get to know each other properly," Janus suggests. "Hello, I'm Janus, owner of Fabrizio's Fabrics and the King of Club Casa de Fuego. I inherited the name of my shop from the former owner, and I'm planning on changing it. I just haven't found the perfect name yet."

"So very nice to meet you, Mr. Janus," I say, curtseying slightly, bringing a smile to Janus's face. "I'm Donnie, on a mission to be a Queen. We have something in common. I'm also searching for the perfect name. Right now, they call me Nadie, literally Nobody. But that fits, I guess, till I find my name."

"Donnie, let me tell you something. I know a lot of Queens. Sometimes, we have to search for our names. But the lucky ones don't have to look for a name. The name finds us."

Carlito peeks from around the corner, jumping into the conversation.

"I told her she should call herself S'mores. 'Cause she always lookin' for S'mores. Get it?"

"Shut up, Lito. You ain't one to be talkin' about gettin' anything. And by the way, did you find the perfect red and black fabrics for me yet? If not, get back to it. We ain't got all day, ya know," I reply.

Janus settles on a stool behind the counter, as I lean in his direction, seeking advice from one I think of as wise.

"Can I ask you a personal question?"

"Of course, child, but before you do, let me give you a little advice, even though you didn't ask for it. I know that both you and Divinity have your eyes on Eliud, and yes, he is a gorgeous boy. But don't let him break up your friendship. He's a player."

"And how would you know that?"

"He told me himself. He wants to be with every Queen in the house. Physical pleasure only. He isn't looking for anything permanent. So think about how much you wanna give to someone who's only looking to take."

I sigh, knowing I'll have to learn this lesson myself. I like Elie a lot, and I'm not ready to give up the chase this soon.

Changing the subject without answering directly, I ask Janus, "How did you select your name? Or did it select you somehow? I'm struggling with mine, and I'd like to know your story."

Suddenly, another interruption.

"Whaddya think about this fabric? Nice, huh?"

It's Whitey and Carlito, with one holding a roll of gorgeous black satin and the other with a bright red blend that sharply contrasts against the black.

"Nice job, babes," I tell them. "Both perfect. Go back and get another red, but make it darker. I'll be able to use the brighter and darker reds with what I got planned."

They head to the back of the shop, while my attention turns back to Janus.

"By the way, do you know the story of how Divinity got her name?" he asks me.

'Honestly, no. She shoulda called herself T-Rex, 'cause she's a man-eater. And a man-thief, too," I snort.

Janus laughs at that. "It isn't only men she steals. She stole her name, too."

That got my interest. Any dirt to be dished about Divinity, well, color me fascinated.

"Yeah, she was gonna name herself The Lavender Scare. Not a bad name, to be honest. But I doubt most people would even get the reference to the old days when Congress was trying to ruin the lives of anyone even suspected of being gay."

I nod as if I have any idea of what Janus is talking about. But Congress, Lavender Scares, what the hell? I have no clue.

"Sounds like she wanted to be a horror character," was the only thought I had on the subject of her name. "Maybe she coulda been the Lavender Screamer, or...I don't know."

"I asked her if she was gonna wear lavender outfits all the time. Or lavender hair?" Janus adds.

"So anyway, one night she was on Queer Mike's podcast, the same night Melba Toasty was on as a guest, too. You know Melba, right? She's on an East Coast tour, and she'll be performing this Friday with a new act, calling herself Melba Toasty and the Kop Tarts. She'll have two backup dancers dressed like cops. I'm pretty sure they'll be stripping down outta their uniforms during the act."

"Cheezits H. Christ! That's gonna be lit!" That's Carlito, always playing his word games. Mostly referencing food, though not always. He's a quick wit, no doubt about that.

"Lito, be quiet. I wanna hear about Divinity Thee Thief!"

Lito and Whitey stand nearby, their arms filled with fabric, as Janus continues.

"Don't go callin' her Divinity Thee Thief and certainly not to her face. She's Divinity Thee Goddess and she has the right to choose her name and be respected for it," Janus admonishes us. "You'll expect the same when you decide on a name for yourself."

I know that's true, so I nod my assent.

"Anyway..." Janus continues, "Mike was chatting with his guests during a break, off the air, and tells this story about the time he dressed in costume for a Halloween party, where he had been proclaimed as Divinity the God. He was parading around the party, dressed like a Greek Muse. Approaching each guest, he would 'divine' their futures, loudly proclaiming them as whores, harlots, and other such creatures."

"So Miss Divinity then decided to make herself a goddess. I have to admit, that's a cool way to choose a name," I reply.

"Of course, Mike wasn't too happy about it, at first. But then he realized that for him, the name was just for one night. But for Divinity, it became her everything, so Mike decided it was cool. And she never

24

would have chosen that name if it wasn't for Queer Mike and his show."

Whitey, placing his fabrics on the counter to be cut, asks if Janus already told his story, about his name.

"Thanks for reminding me," Janus replies. "If you know the stories of the Roman gods, you might know about Janus."

All this talk about gods. I guess that's a good source for names, but I don't think it suits me at all.

I listen as Janus describes his namesake as the Roman god of transitions and dualities, beginning and endings, often depicted with two faces, each looking in opposite directions.

"Since I was a child, I knew that my spirit didn't match how I was being raised. I went through a lot of anguish, trying to figure myself out. You see the result of all that here in front of you. I chose this name because I want to at least acknowledge both my past life and my present one. This name reminds me where I came from and that's why the name Janus suits me perfectly."

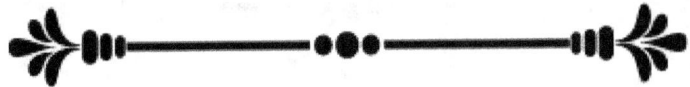

I have a lot to think about. Janus has inspired me to give some real thought to my name.

We spend the rest of the day shopping for accessories for possible future costumes. Our favorite place for that is Party City, located in a strip mall in South Philly, near 24th Street and Passyunk Avenue. Our shopping baskets are filled with trinkets, beads, bows, ribbons, and all sorts of fancy, colorful goodies. Just before we get to the register, I spy a big display with Halloween leftovers at 75% off. I grab a pumpkin necklace, a skeleton bracelet, devil horns and some vampire fangs, at the last minute. You never know when you might need something unusual and I want to be prepared.

Exiting the store, carrying more bags than I expected, we head for the bus stop to return to Center City to catch the El.

"Do we need a few more makeup items?" I ask, eyeing the CVS just across the street. "Can a gurl ever have too much lipstick and mascara?"

"Hun, we got the whole *kitten-ka-booty* back at the house," Lito replies.

"The whole what?" asks Whitey, rolling his eyes as I'm ready to roll over laughing.

"You know, the *kitten-ka-booty*. It's like when you already got all you need."

Laughing, we get on the bus, that just pulled up to the stop. *Kitten-ka-booty*. What the hell?!

It's dusk by the time we get to our stop, Allegheny. Whitey had gotten off at the previous stop, Somerset, because he was meeting up with one of his local subscribers from OnlyFans. That left us with even more bags to carry ourselves.

We're only halfway down the first block of our walk home when I stop suddenly, seeing the sight I've dreaded the most, and the one I never want Lito to see.

Our Kensington neighborhood has been hit hard by the opioid epidemic, with several homeless encampments within just a few blocks. But as fentanyl-laced drugs were causing major problems in other parts of the country, Philly, and particularly Kensington, was experiencing something far more sinister.

Tranq.

Sounds kind of harmless, right? Maybe you're thinking of tranquility, or *tranquilo*. But no, this is the street name for the animal tranquilizer xylazine, that's being mixed with fentanyl, inflicting users with large wounds that won't heal. Infections are widespread among users, with many needing to have body parts amputated.

And the smell—the disgusting smell of rotting human flesh envelopes the area where users congregate. Users desperate for a fix, and willing to do whatever it takes to get what they need.

It isn't hard to spot tranq addicts. Besides the awful smell, they are afflicted with what's called the "tranq walk," where they look like zombies, totally unaware of their surroundings. Or, they stand swaying in one spot, with their body bent almost in half, their faces practically touching their shoes.

What stops me isn't the sight of a group of addicts, though. It's one particular person, identifiable by her dress, which I had given to her as a gift a few Christmases ago. Even with her head hanging low, her face covered by her drooping hair, there was no mistake.

It's Mami. I don't want Lito to see her like that. Grabbing hold of his arm, I say, "I forgot, we need some rice from the bodega. We're all out," and I drag him in the opposite direction.

He gives no indication that he'd seen Mami, but I'm not sure. I want Carlito to think of Mami the way she used to be, and maybe how she'll be again, if she gets the right treatment.

Protecting my brother is all I can think of right now. We'll find a different route home.

PRIDEZILLA

Considering I'm making a life-changing move, I feel relaxed as I board the train from Baltimore to Philly. Finding a window seat is a blessing; I'm looking forward to enjoying the sights as we make our way out of Maryland and into Pennsylvania.

My long legs are cramped into the small space, so I'm hoping that no one will take the seat next to me.

"Please be sure all bags are placed in the overhead racks. This train is completely sold out and every available seat will be needed for passengers," comes the announcement from the unseen conductor.

Damn! There goes that idea. Reluctantly, I grab the bag I had placed on the seat next to mine, hoping to avoid unwanted contact with a stranger on the train.

At least I'll be able to ignore them by either staring out the window or scrolling through my phone.

I've traveled by train more than a few times, and it's always been my experience that the very large Black man sitting by himself (*that would be me*) is always the last choice for fellow travelers to sit next to. Add to that my clearly apparent femininity, and it was a foregone conclusion that the seat next to mine would be the last to be taken, if at all.

I have a habit of judging people as they pass by, scanning the car for available seats.

Honey, I wish. I could toast his buns for hours, I think, as a young, white, most definitely gay prettyboy sashays right on by, while I admire his considerable *ASSets.*

The middle-aged business suits would rather stand in the next car than take the empty seat next to me.

My gaze is momentarily distracted by a minor commotion on the boarding track, as an older man in a wheelchair loudly protests that he needs to be seated as close as possible to the exit door.

Must be a newbie, I'm thinking about the Amtrak employee, seemingly unaware of the need for accommodations for disabled individuals.

Those thoughts are interrupted by the sighing of a woman lowering herself carefully into the seat next to mine.

"You okay, hon?" I ask politely. "Need anything?"

"Don't mind me, Sonny. I do just fine by myself. Just getting a little up there in years, so I gotta be careful not to break a hip each time I change my position!"

Her laughter assures me that she's joking. Maybe the trip won't be all that unpleasant after all.

I lean back against the window of the car, trying to get a better look at my traveling companion. Elderly, but I can tell that she knows how to care for herself, with just enough make-up to enhance her delicate features, a nicely-tailored business suit paired with sensible shoes, and a small pocketbook slung over her shoulder.

One potential problem. Her choice of perfume. *What is that, Eau de Costco?* was my unkind assessment. I could only hope that my ability to smell the noxious odor would fade quickly. Very quickly.

"Oh, I called you, Sonny. Perhaps I misjudged. I'm so very sorry," she says, as she lightly touches my left hand, noticing my exquisitely manicured nails polished in a blood-red background with intricate zodiac designs done in white.

"What shall I call you, my beautiful friend?" she asks, and my heart melts at the kindness emanating from this complete stranger.

"I'd like to share a secret with you," I whisper in a tone that can only be described as conspiratorial.

"Please do!" she smiles back.

"My real name, the one that defines me, is..."

She laughs as I hesitate, pretending to divulge something dark and sinister.

"Spill the tea, my darling. My ears are just dying to hear it now!" she whispers back.

"I have a stage name. I'm an actress. And my name is Pridezilla, but off stage, I'm Jalen."

The sparkle in her eyes brightens as I take note of her incredible smile.

"Pridezilla! Just a moment, let me think..."

Now, it was her turn to tease me about her reaction to my secret.

"That name is brilliant. It's layered with meaning, am I right?" She continues speaking, without waiting for a reply.

"I can just picture you up on the stage, in what I would guess are some fabulous costumes. Oh my gosh, I feel so happy today! Years and years ago, my brother used to perform as a drag queen. His name was..."

Her story is interrupted as the conductor asks for our tickets. She hands him a paper ticket, and then I flash my phone at him so he can confirm that I am indeed a paying customer.

How cute and quaint, I think of her old-fashioned ways, as the conductor places color-coded tickets in the slots on top of the chairs in front of us.

"We're both going to Philly, I see," I say to her, seeing that our ticket colors matched.

"Yes, I was just visiting my sister for a few days in Baltimore. She hasn't been well recently, so I came down from Philly for a visit."

"Oh!" she continues. "I have to apologize if you've noticed a certain ...well...odor. My sister has the worst taste. She bought me a thank-you gift for visiting her, and before I left, she practically showered me with this; well, let's just call it what it is. A cheap drug-store brand of what's supposed to pass for perfume. I tried to wash it off, but..."

"No worries," I assure her. "But I'm glad to know that wasn't your choice of what to wear. It's positively odious."

We laugh and relax in the company of one another.

My thoughts travel to my hopes for the future, moving to a new city, into a new relationship, trying to relieve my concerns by concentrating on the beautiful scenery outside. A far cry from inner-city Baltimore, which I desperately needed to leave. Desperate enough to accept an invitation from a total stranger on Grindr, hoping he might be the key to a brighter future.

I hope he's using real photos on his profiles there, I think. *And if they are real, I hope they aren't like 10 or 20 years old.*

It's commonly reported among train travelers that time seems motionless for many while they ride the rails. For me, it's slightly different. I experience a rare form of time blindness. Time does stand still, but then it also gets disjointed, so my memories of train trips are muddled and non-synchronous. Something in my mind breaks these moments into tiny pieces, without any regular order.

These fragments of time become shredded, like a particularly disturbing dream.

One minute, my newfound lady friend is chatting with me. A moment later, she's asleep, her head resting against my shoulder as she snores ever so quietly. Our conversations are jumbled in my mind, as I struggle to remember the proper sequence, though I do remember the details. And isn't that all that matters in the end?

When I get into my Uber at 30th Street Station in Philly, on my way to my future at 12th and Morris Streets, I'm thinking about what happened on the train.

"My name's Ruby," I remember being told. "My brother was Rudy, but the funny thing is, he was also called Rubee."

Ah yes, I smile to myself. *Her name's Ruby and her brother, named Rudy, used Rubee Red Lips as his drag name.*

"At family gatherings, when someone called 'Ruby!' both of us would answer," she had laughed.

Showing her the photos of the man I was moving in with, she noted, "Oh my! I have my doubts about those. Look at that one where he's standing outside the Westbury Bar. But that bar closed years ago. I don't remember the exact date, maybe 2013 or 14. And so that photo, where the bar is clearly in business, is at least 9 or 10 years old. Maybe much older."

My heart sank as she spoke. My Grindr "savior," who was promising me a bright future in a new city, might not be the knight in shining armor I was hoping for.

I wish I could remember everything from the train sequentially, but it's like I'm reading index cards that were scattered on the floor, now needing to be rearranged into the proper order.

As the driver turns right onto one of the numbered streets, my mind becomes crowded with memories of my conversation with Ruby. I was seeing speech bubbles, like those you see in comic books, containing the dialogue of the characters. For me, the bubbles burst, spilling the remnants of the conversation throughout the surrounding air, but in no particular order.

"Rudy always wore sparkly dresses, almost always in red."

"Did you do your nails yourself? I'm fascinated!"

"If you have any trouble in Philly, contact me and let me know."

"Yes, I would design and sew Rubee's dresses. He adored my designs."

I made a mental note of the pronoun-switching and figured it was natural for her to refer to her drag queen brother as both a he and a she.

"Yes, Rubee wore the reddest lipstick we could find, hence the name," she laughed.

"Do you know the song 'Jungle Fever?'"

Did I answer her? I struggle to remember.

More remnants, out of order.

"I live in a small condo on Rittenhouse Square. Ever hear of it?"

"Oh yes, Stevie Wonder! He had a soundtrack album for the movie *Jungle Fever*." I did reply to her question. I smile with satisfaction at the memory.

"No, honey, no, no, no." Pursing her lips, she reached for her phone, went straight to YouTube and played the version of "Jungle Fever" released by The Chakachas in 1970. We both bounced along to the beat in our seats as she explained.

"This was the final song played in every performance by Rudy. Just picture a tall, skinny drag queen with an angular face, sometimes with a bit of a 5 o'clock shadow peeking out from under a ton of foundation, and the brightest red lips you can imagine."

I had a vivid picture in my mind.

"After lip-syncing a few songs, 'Jungle Fever' would begin. That's when Rubee would go out into the audience, find the cutest young twink he could in the audience, and drag him up onto the stage."

Audience participation—one of the keys to success in a performance.

She was laughing, fondly recalling her brother's drag shows.

"Sometimes, the boy was planted in advance, but not always. It was more fun when a random cutie was plucked from the crowd, brought up on the stage, as Rubee danced lasciviously around him, to this very song."

The lyrics, mostly consisting of sounds of sexual passion, struck me as a perfect song for some very sexy moves onstage.

"And as the song continued, Rubee would simulate having sex with the twink, ending in a long, drawn-out licking of her middle finger and then pretending to penetrate his fine, fat ass with the wet digit. Oh, the crowd just loved it!"

"Play it again," I ask her. "I never heard this one before."

Remembering the train ride, I can hear the song begin, picturing myself paying homage to Rubee Red Lips, recreating her performance from so many years ago.

As the Uber nears our destination, I search YouTube, playing the song to myself through my AirBuds, wondering if a modern audience would like it.

When the driver pulls to the side to drop me off, one final speech bubble pops open in my head.

I both see and hear Ruby saying, "I hope we get together sometime. I have the most fabulous fabric store where I'd like to go shopping with you. It's called Fabrizio's."

ENCOUNTERS

"You want Cheery Hoes this morning?" Carlito asks me, waving a box of cereal in the air.

I nod, laughing, but Lito's back is turned to me, so he thinks I didn't answer.

"Speak now or forever hold your Reese's Pieces!" he shouts.

"Hold on, lil man. What's this?" I ask, turning his head with my hand to get a better look at the giant hickey on his neck.

Pulling his head away, avoiding direct eye contact, Lito confesses.

"I kissed a boy last night!"

"Kissed? Maybe you kissed him, but it looks like he took a bite outta you!"

"Awwwwww," Carlito struggles to find a reply.

"Did he have fangs? I mean, damn!"

Lito maintains his silence as he pours OJ, coffee, and then the milk over our cereal.

"He's a nice guy and we had a little fun," he finally replies.

"Oh honey, I probably shouldn't joke with you. This is a big step," I laugh. "You made it all the way to first base, and with a boy! Congrats to you," I say, raising my glass of OJ as if making a toast.

"More like third base," he murmurs.

"I heard that, you sly dog," I try to say, crunching on a mouthful of Cheery Hoes.

I give my little brother a knowing wink. "Tell me all about it when you're ready to talk."

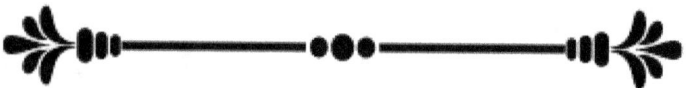

I have to make a living since I support both myself and my little brother. Rent, food, clothing—it all adds up fast! So, I do what I have to do.

People might think I blow my money on non-essentials, such as make-up, wigs, fabric for costumes, high heels, trips to the manicure shop, etc. But for me, those items are essentials. Without them, I don't know what my reason would be for living. Don't pass judgment too quickly.

Today is manicure day. Whitey and I have a standing appointment at Genesis Nail Salon on Girard Avenue every other Wednesday at 2 PM.

"Hello, Myeong, my darling!" I call, taking one of the face masks available at the counter. "You look stunning today, honey!"

Whitey struts up to Na-Rae's station, giving his standard air kisses, exclaiming for everyone to hear, "I have to look extra-fabulous today, doll. I wanna impress my date tonight so fancy me up! He has high expectations, you know!"

The regular customers pay us no mind as we carry on, camping it up as we chat, all four of us, about the latest celebrity gossip. Girl talk. Just like we always do.

"Whitey, did you hear any news about what's goin' on between Rachel and Bryan? I mean, if you can't find true love on *The Bachelorette*, then where's a girl supposed to look?" Our cackles fill the room, as we enjoy serving the dish.

About five minutes into our manis, I hear it—the cough. You know the one I mean. The cough someone makes when they disapprove of something, and they're just dying to tell you about it.

Looking in the direction of the sound, I see the disapproving eyes of a white woman, scowling directly at me.

I stare right back. Then I do the same cough, with my patented head shake, right at her.

That sets her off. "Why are you calling him 'Whitey'? You got something against white people? I'm sick and tired of this reverse discrimination against decent white folks," she steams.

Turning her attention to Whitey, raising her voice in indignation, she fumes, "And why are you sitting there just taking it? Speak up for yourself! Don't let anyone call you a whitey, and let them get away with it!"

Knowing that the woman completely misunderstood what she heard did not make me feel any forgiveness for her. I wasn't one to let people try to publicly chastise me, especially when all they're really doing is sticking their nose into my private business.

Glaring in her direction, raising my hands into a claw-like position, and raising myself in an aggressive stance, I verbally pounce at her.

"Listen, lady," I tell her. "I don't know who you think you is, but you're just another pushy white lady to me."

Turning to my friends, I continue, "I bet her name's Karen. Ain't that right, Karen? Always trying to put us brown people down!"

I start to remove my earrings, a sure sign of a fight in my neighborhood.

"Stop it, ladies—all of you. We aren't having no fights up in here. The first one to throw a punch gets kicked out, kicked out for good!"

Genesis, the salon owner, intervenes just in time to stop me from taking that lady out. And I don't mean out for dinner!

Huffing as I return to my seat, I loudly announce that I'll be changing my regular appointment time, in order to avoid ever seeing "Karen" again.

Then I turn my attention back to my nails and our conversation, as if nothing at all had happened.

Though I have no set schedule, each day flies by as I watch Drag Queen makeup tutorials on YouTube, chat with friends, go shopping, and do anything else to keep a young femme like me busy. Quite often, I'm confronted with the need to make some cash, and today is one of those days.

"I'm looking for right now," I type into my phone, knowing that plenty of guys on Grindr will be looking for what I'm offering. Then

I add "3oo only," meaning that I'm expecting at least $300 cash for my services. You have to trick the bots patrolling Grindr, looking for anyone violating their terms of service, so I avoid using actual numbers that might be noticed and get me kicked off the app.

Two replies appear almost immediately.

"Hot pix," a guy with no screen name or photo writes. "Looking for a panty boy. Red or pink panties."

"Suck my big dick," is the other reply, from an older man with a moustache.

I reply to the guy looking for service from a panty boy. That's exactly my style. We arrange to meet at his place.

An hour later, my mouth stuffed with cock, I sit spread-eagled on the floor, allowing my mind to wander as I work my magic tongue and lips on his hardness. Not paying attention to the task at hand causes me to use just a little too much teeth on him.

"Damn, bitch, watch your mouth. Don't be fanging me with those teeth. You're such a pretty boy, especially when you wear them damn panties. I'd hate to have to fuck up your face."

I guess the thought of giving a beating to a gurl like me pushes him over the edge. He shoots off into my mouth and down my throat.

Two seconds later, he commands me to get dressed and get out.

"My wife's gonna be home soon. If you ever see me with her any-where, we don't know each other, you got that?"

He dresses quickly, as do I.

"Don't get me wrong, I needed that. My wife refuses to suck my dick, so sometimes I need a pretty panty boy to give me some head. Maybe we'll do it again sometime."

He pats my behind as he guides me towards the door.

Hesitating for a brief moment, he realizes what he has to do. I don't have to tell him that if he doesn't pay, I'll be standing right here arguing with him when his unsuspecting wife gets home. He pays the bill and I'm out the door.

SISTERS, SISTERS

This Friday night, the line to get into Fuego is three blocks long. Everyone knows that Melba Toasty and the Kop Tarts are scheduled to put on a show.

I didn't see any fliers around the hood about this event, but word does have a way of traveling fast in these parts, so it seems that all those who love the Drag Queens somehow know and they're all expecting a good time tonight.

I'm at my usual spot on the balcony, sipping my gin 'n' tonic, watching Divinity Thee Goddess chatting it up with Eliud. On the inside, I'm seething, though on the outside, I'm cold as ice.

The opening act is just getting started, warming up the audience for tonight's stars.

The Two Vs, aka Vageena and Virginny are making their debut at Fuego, and finding some new fans. Even from a distance, it's apparent that they need to work on their makeup skills. But that's typical when Queens are just getting started. What looks good in the dressing room doesn't always work on the stage.

"Givin' them props for those outfits, though the makeup looks crazy," Whitey says, as if he had read my mind about the makeup. "They got the dresses almost exactly like in the movie, and where the hell did they get those fab feathery fans?"

The Two Vs, as they had been introduced, were lip-syncing the song "Sisters," as performed by Rosemary Clooney and Vera-Ellen in that old classic movie, *White Christmas*.

Though the club patrons are mostly Black and Latino, it isn't unusual to have white Queens performing. While I had never seen this particular song performed before, it didn't strike me as out-of-place, particularly since the movie is so well-known. Performers often sing classics, though the younger Queens usually perform more current hits.

Exiting to raucous applause and a shower of bills, this particular set of "Sisters" had made a good impression at the club.

The Snark Sharks enjoyed the act, but were quick to critique their look. Ru-Barb and Nepharious were joined tonight by Ritzy Quackers and Glamazon.

Ru-Barb: "Serving cuntiness supreme, with a side dish of, oh, I don't know, vaginity, I think!"

Glamazon: "These sisters are A-listers! Love the song, and honey, I am adoring those cute outfits! But ladies, who did their eyes? Alice

Cooper? I mean, their eyes looked like a kid just made a finger painting on their faces."

Ritzy Quackers: "The outfits are insane. They lined their ducks up in a row, and I thought they were ritzilicious! But you're right about the makeup. It's like, Duck, Duck, Goose Egg!"

Nepharious: "I love the song choice, and the dance routine is right out of the movie. Perfectly done. But Antoine," she says, turning her head to Ru-Barb, with one finger on her chin," What do we think of the makeup?"

"Well, Blaine, I think we can agree that we both..." and then they say in unison, "HATED IT!"

Using the "Hated It" line from the "Men On Film" skits, featured years ago on *In Living Color* is a favorite of these two Queens, always good for huge laughs.

While a technical issue delays the start of the next act, I see Ru-Barb gesturing, inviting me over to her seat.

"Why my little SnapDragon, whatever did you mean by snapping at me last week?"

"I am so sorry. I was in a mood that night, and wasn't really thinkin'. Kinda drunk, too."

Pursing her lips as only she could, Ru replies, "Not much of an excuse, child. Especially when I hear you're thinking of taking the stage. And with a face like yours, it's possible you could be a superstar."

"I promise it won't happen again," I reply.

"And just 'cause you're beautiful, that don't give you the right to diss those who came before you," Nepharious adds. "With that negativity, you'll find your fans might end up snappin' at you, Miss Fanny Snapper! Is that what you want?"

"No ma'am...I mean, no, your Nephariousness, I don't want that for sure." My comment causes the entire group of Snark Sharks to cluck and laugh.

"Now begone child! Watch and learn. These Queens tonight have a few things to teach ya!"

My attention, however, wanders back to Divinity and Eliud at the bar. *I despise that bitch*; I'm thinking, when Whitey suddenly says, "Do you think she had a point?"

I scrunch my face as if I had just bitten into the lime in my drink.

"What did Divinity say about me this time?"

"Not Divinity, Donnie. The lady in the nail shop. Did she have a point, what she was tellin' us?"

I don't have time to answer before Sir Janus begins stirring up the crowd with an introduction for the next act.

"Ladies, ladies, and ladies," he jokes. "And the rest of you whatevers, you absolutely beautiful Queers, your King is in need of your attention!"

"Here I stand, Janus the Great, your Drag King Extraordinaire, here to announce the HOTTEST show Fuego has ever seen. Coming directly to you, all the way from the great L.A., Los Angeles, California, the act voted the Most Drag-a-licious Threesome, the group that's gonna LIGHT your FIYA!"

"Here they are, Melba Toasty and the Kop Tarts!"

Forgetting about Divinity, Eliud and even Whitey for the moment, I'm captivated by the show, which literally starts with a bang.

Fireworks are set off on the sides of the stage, and twirling sparklers keep the fiery atmosphere ablaze. The curtains part, revealing the guys known as the Kop Tarts already on the stage, dressed in something close to cop uniforms. Though no one could mistake these men for the real police, with fringe added to the uniforms, the backs of the trousers are cut-out, open shirts displaying the harnesses worn around their upper bodies, and sexy makeup on their faces. Those cops could haul me in on any trumped-up charge, and I'd be one happy gurl. They're dancing and twirling to a heavy, hypnotic beat.

All eyes are on Melba as she enters, dramatically wheeled onto center stage inside a cage, handcuffed to the sides and dressed in a spectacular, fiery orange costume, all glitter and sparkle, and wearing one of the longest blonde wigs I've ever seen. Wildly tossing her hair in a circular motion, writhing as if trying to escape from her imprisonment, I think she captured the heart of everyone in the audience who had ever felt trapped, including those who had actually experienced being in prison.

Melba is well-known for her activism for social justice, always fighting for the rights of the LGBTQ+ community. So maybe I should have been better prepared for what happens next.

The heavy beat of the instrumental track stops suddenly. Melba stands motionless for a moment, and her gogo boys, the Kops, stand still, facing in her direction.

The music track heads in a completely different direction, with Melba singing a soulful ballad, "Freedom," which features Queen Latifah, Mary J. Blige, TLC and Aaliyah.

When the track reaches the part with the background chorus singing, I'm feeling the emotions. Then we suddenly witness the Kops draw pistols from their holsters, aim directly at Melba, and hear multiple shots fired.

I'm caught completely off guard. First, just hearing the sound of gunfire inside our club immediately brings the massacres at Pulse nightclub in Orlando, and more recently at Club Q in Colorado Springs, to mind. Watching Melba slump to the floor, with her arms held high by the cuffs restraining her, makes me gasp. Her hair falls in front of her, completely hiding her face, as the sickening scent from the gunshots engulf me.

Total silence for five full seconds.

Melba is using her art to remind us of the horrors suffered by people just like us, in a place just like this.

Knowing how to work a crowd, Melba slowly begins to rise to her full height of 5 feet 8 inches, with another 6 inches added by her stiletto heels.

The Kops open the gate to the cage, then release Melba from her shackles. At that point, she leaps from the cage, leaving behind her costume and wig, which had been rigged to tear away at this exact moment.

Once again, the music blares as the Kops tear away their uniforms, revealing their sparkly string thongs with extra-large packaging in the front.

Damn, what I wouldn't give to take a bite out of one of those King-Size Tarts, I remember thinking.

Song Number Two is a guaranteed hit with this crowd, an anthem of overcoming adversity known to all. Melba gives the full dramatic treatment to "I Will Survive" by Gloria Gaynor.

Her second outfit of the night is a violet gown emblazoned with lightning bolts, her hair a mix of bluish hues, and one of the Kops places a tiara on the head of the Queen, entertaining us with one of the most uplifting songs ever recorded.

Melba gracefully accepts handfuls of cash from her adoring fans as she crosses the stage majestically.

And then in a flash, she changes her appearance once more, right in front of our eyes. Her boy toys, carefully chosen for their astounding looks and physiques, tug at her dress, pulling it away, revealing the final outfit, the same lacy lingerie worn by Gaga in her "Bad Romance" video.

The performance for this song, matching the video, is high energy, raw, sexy and confident, as Melba and the Kop Tarts are perfectly synchronized during their erotic dance.

Then, as her dancers depart, Melba takes her place at the center of the stage, a lone spotlight on her, as she performs her finale, "Lacy" by Olivia Rodrigo. The performance is tender, sweet, and lovely.

I went home alone that night, having a lot to ponder.

And all night long, I dreamt of stardom.

FANGULA

"Mornin' Donnie! We all out of Grape Smuts this morning, but I got some creme-filled donuts for breakfast today. You want one?"

"One? Who you jokin' with? I'll take three!"

I don't know how Carlito does it, getting up early each morning, preparing breakfast, pouring the coffee. And always ready with some corny-ass jokes to brighten my day.

"Look what I got last night!"

I almost gag on the pastry when he shows me his new tattoo, still fresh and a little bloody, needing time to heal.

"It's a cobra! Ain't he a beauty?"

"Wow! They did great work. Look at the details!" I admire the intricacies of the artist's design.

"Who did it for you?"

"You know Liphe from over on Madison? He did it and for half price."

"He did a full forearm for half price? Ohhh, somebody must be likin' you," I tease.

Lito's face turns red, and I know I'm right.

"So, I been thinkin'," Lito says, changing the subject. "I'm gettin' tired of always bein' called Little Lito or Car-Car or even Carlito. I need a real nick. One that fits me. So I'm thinkin' about tellin' everybody to call me Cobra. Whatcha think?"

Looking up at Lito, with a smile on my face, I know he's attempting to find himself; to figure out who he is and how he fits into the world.

"I like it, Cobra," I tell him, giving my blessing by using his new name. "Just one question. Was your little snake pointing up and spreading out like a cobra when you got this idea?" I like to tease my brother about liking boys.

Ignoring my question, Cobra continues, "Check out these fangs. Drippin' blood. That part adds drama, right there!"

Stuffing the last bit of my third donut into my mouth, I start thinking about fangs. Where did I hear that before?

Then, the memory hits me hard. The dude I was sucking off told me not to use my fangs. And the last thing I picked up during a recent shopping trip was a set of costume fangs. And now Lito...I mean, Cobra...is talking about fangs. Coincidence?

Then, I remember the words of advice that Janus had given me back at the fabric store.

Sometimes, we have to search for our names. But the lucky ones don't have to look. The name finds us.

So what am I supposed to choose? Fangtastic? Fangulosity? Fang Fang? Fangula?

Hmmmm, Fangula. That one is giving me something to chew on. Or does it sound too much like a character from a horror movie?

I take a minute to think, then make a decision. I'm going to be Fangula! Why? First, the name is calling out to me. Second, it's fabulously fierce. And third, it goes against type. Lots of times, pretty ones like me select pretty names. I don't want that. Different and original is more my style. Decision made. Fangula, it is!

"Cobra, you're a genius! You just helped me find my drag name. Or, I should say, you helped my drag name find me. Get ready to meet the Fabulous, the Fierce, the Ferocious...FANGULA!"

I practically run over to Whitey's house, at least as fast as I can in these shoes. I have to tell him about my new name, my new drag identity. I know he'll be just as excited as I am.

Making my way from "G" Street to his house on "H" Street, I run down the narrow, curved alleyway behind the small cottages on E. Madison Street, lined with trash cans, making the Sign of the Cross as I see Jamal's kicks dangling from the overhead phone lines, commemorating his short, violent life. I make the sign every time I pass this spot, where he'd been gunned down in the midst of a gang war. Jamal was my friend back at Clemente Middle School, and I miss his laughter and jokes.

Jamal never knew about my impure thoughts as I'd watch him run the court during gym class, seeing the glossy sweat on his sinewy arms, hearing the screech of his kicks as he pulled up for a jump-shot, his extra-long, satin b-ball shorts flapping as they sagged from his slim hips. And that boy had mad skills. I always thought he'd be one to escape the hood and maybe make it all the way to the NBA.

Every time I pass by this spot, it seems that there's a sound, a buzzing, in the air. Sometimes, I imagine that Jamal is trying to send me a message, but that can't be possible, can it? Maybe I'm just not listening hard enough.

The trilling of birds captures my attention and I notice a pair of cardinals nesting on top of the pole nearest to Jamal's sneakers. The crimson male flies to the ground and approaches me. I wish I had something to offer, so I start searching through my bag.

It chirps at me. "Purty, purty, purty!"

"Well then, you do have good taste!" I say as the bird looks at me, cocking his head from side to side.

I wonder if Jamal would have ever thought of me as being "purty."

Then, I find what I'm looking for, the pack of sunflower seeds. I toss a few in the direction of this beautiful bird. He looks at me, shakes his head, and takes a seed. He flies up to his mate, feeding her. I have no way to tell if eggs are in the nest, but I hope they'll soon be proud parents.

My gaze returns to the kicks and, though the elements have taken their toll, I can still see where Jamal's uncle had used a black Sharpie to write his name on the back of the sneakers.

Jamal, just another candle extinguished all too soon, only remembered now as a pair of lonely sneakers, dangling, tossing in the morning breeze.

"Whitey, Whitey, I've got great news! Remember when Janus said that I'd find my drag name?"

"Course I do. From the look on your face, I think you found it, right?"

"Kinda. The truth is, it was more like the opposite. I went searching for my drag name, but my name found me."

Whitey looks at me like he's about to burst with excitement.

"This morning, Cobra was showing me his new tatt..."

"Cobra? Who the hell is Cobra?"

"Oh, that's Lito's new name. That's part of what I'm tryin' to tell ya. Lito got a new name, and now he's Cobra. It fits him good, I think, right?"

The words were tumbling out of my mouth faster than I could manage.

"And then he was talkin' about the fangs on his tatt, and I remembered the dude that told me to watch my fangs when I was suckin' him off and plus we bought a set of fangs over at the CVS, you remember all that, right?"

"Hold on, Donnie. You sucked a guy and he was bitchin' about your fangs? What the holy hell?"

"Never mind all that. I'll give you the deets later. My point is, the word FANG kept coming up to me all day. That's how my name found me. It jumped right into my head. Here I am, the one and only, the fabulous, the ferocious...you ready?"

"Tell me, gurl!"

"FANGULA! Ain't that just so purrrrrfect?"

A look of hesitation momentarily comes over Whitey's face. *Oh no, he doesn't even like it. And I was so excited. I thought it was goddamn perfect.*

Then slowly, Whitey's face widens into the biggest grin I've ever seen.

"Fangula, Fangula, Fangula...we all bow down to the Queen...the fiercest and the fairest in the land...Fangula! I fuckin' LOVE it!" he shouts, grabbing me into a bear hug so tight I almost couldn't breathe.

My plan is to spend the day watching YouTube drag queen makeup videos, knowing I have to improve my skills. I haven't posted any new videos on my channel for a few weeks, mostly because no one's watching them. It's discouraging, but I still want to make my mark on YouTube.

TikTok is easier. I can just dance, dressed commando-style, wearing something that shows my freak swingin' and swayin'. That's always good for hundreds, sometimes thousands of views. I know why guys watch those videos, because I watch them for hours, too, but I want to be known for something more than that.

"Wanna watch me showin' off my floppy disk?" I ask Whitey.

"Hell no!" he laughs. "Don't be swingin' your stick in my face!"

"I meant on video; I just uploaded a new one last night. You know how the guys always comment that they're surprised that mine is an extra large."

"I know, Donnie...I mean, Fangula, but we both know which one of us got the real *bicho grande*."

Giggles galore fill the small room.

"Don't you think you should text Janus to see if he can fit you into the show on Friday? You know, it isn't like there's any lack of queens who wanna be up on that stage each week."

Whitey's right. I send a quick text, expecting an immediate reply, but nothing comes.

"I wanna ask you something. You said Lito changed his name to Cobra today, right?"

I nod.

"And you have a new drag name, starting today. You want me to call you Fangy now, or something like that?"

"No, dude, I'm still Donnie. Fangula's my stage name. You already know that."

"So, with everybody getting new names, I'm still thinking about the lady at the nail shop saying I shouldn't be called Whitey."

"Why do you care what some rando thinks? She ain't nobody."

"But that's just it. She might be a rando, but she said in words what I've been thinkin' about for a while. Whitey was a cool name for a long time, but I don't think I want that name for my whole life."

"So now you wanna be called...what? Franklin? Frankie? Frank? Maybe Frankfurter. You wanna be the hot dog now, right?"

"Shut up," he tells me. "Why is it no problem for you and Lito to change your names like you change your panties, but then you gonna give me grief over me changin' mine? Where in the hell is the sense in that?"

Pursing my lips, I start to give him hell, but then I stop myself.

Why should anyone have a name imposed on them? We get named by our parents, and some people like the choice that was made, and others don't. Shouldn't everyone be able to pick a name they like?

"Ok, you're right. What did you decide on?" I ask.

"That's just it. I can't think of one, and I've been tryin' for a few days already. Can you help me?"

"Sure, Whi...I mean, Frank...ah hell, what am I supposed to call you until we pick one?" I ask.

"I'm still Whitey till we figure something out, I guess. But for now, I gotta go get ready. This Bandana Boy is doing a live show on my OnlyFans tonight. I'm expecting a big crowd and I really need the cash."

I know Whitey does a show, billing himself as Bandana Boy. He always wears a bandana around his neck when he's performing. It's part of his online identity, but it all started when he decided to cover up the neck scar he has as a result of a knife attack when he was a kid.

I head home, still waiting for a reply from Janus about the show on Friday.

TWIGGY

I'm a little nervous, standing on the porch at 1273 Morris Street, staring at the ornate door, my eyes wandering to the intricate patterns of plants and flowers on display in the picture window. I can hear the shuffling steps approach as my new... friend?... roommate?... lover?...neared the door.

"Welcome, Jalen!" He almost trips on the interior doormat as he reaches to embrace all 6 feet 3 inches, 240 pounds of me.

Gently, I return the gesture, fearing that too much pressure might cause me to break a nail—or this slender, older man in front of me.

"Come in, come in, my dear! You look so lovely!"

A compliment always brings a smile to my face.

I leave my rolling suitcase in the foyer, following Victor into the living room, where I sit, holding my handbag on my lap.

Thoughts twirl in my mind.

When did his hair turn white?

Why is he so thin?

His cheeks are naturally rosy. I'd kill for that!

"I know you must be wondering, so let me explain a little," he starts.

"Oh no, there's no need!" I protest.

"Hush, hush. Now that you see me in person, I hope you don't hate me for using such old photos on my profile. I realize I've changed a bit."

A bit? I thought. *Now, that's an understatement.*

"When you told me you were looking for a fresh start, I was interested right away. I've always enjoyed the company of younger men, and to be honest, you're my type. My sexual type, I mean. But if you're not interested in me that way, I'm okay with being friends. I'll leave that up to you."

I wasn't expecting him to say that.

"I've lost a lot of weight, but it's been on purpose. As a matter of fact, my friends have started calling me Twiggy, like the supermodel."

"Oh yes, Twiggy!" I murmur. "She was so influential."

I make a mental note to google this Twiggy person as soon as I have a moment alone, having no idea who he or she is...or was.

"You can call me Twiggy, if you like," Victor purrs, trying to sound like a sexy supermodel.

Without answering, I think, *I wonder if Twiggy spoke like that?*

"We'll have something to eat right after you get settled in. Go ahead, take your bags up to your room and unpack. Then I'll give you the full guided tour."

Marching up the steep stairway, I'm already feeling comfortable here. Mostly because he told me that sex won't be a requirement. I do not find Victor to be attractive at all.

"Can we meet up sometime soon? I need to talk to somebody I can trust. This is me from the train. Hope you remember."

I hit Send, attaching a photo to the text message, hoping that Ruby will see it. With people her age, you can't be too sure about their tech skills. I hope I won't have to make an actual phone call.

The reply is immediate, bringing a sense of relief, knowing we can communicate quickly and easily.

"Of course, honey. And I remember you. Pridezilla."

"Yes, that's me. Did I ever tell you my real name? Jalen."

"Jalen it is. Got it. Free for lunch tomorrow?"

We make plans to meet at The Garden of Eden, a popular gathering spot for those who enjoy being seen, including social media influencers. TikTokers are creating videos, using ring lights to enhance their images, as I brush past the outdoor seating area, to meet Ruby inside.

It would be an understatement to say I was impressed with her, seated regally at the table with the very best view in the house, dressed in a show of impeccable taste. The double string of pearls around her neck perfectly accessorized the designer suit, its light lavender color matching her Louboutins.

"I'm sorry," I apologize. "I didn't know about the dress code here."

"Don't be silly. You're fine. Do you do your own makeup? It brings out your beauty in a subtle way that I find intriguing. I assume this is your daytime look, not your stage makeup," she giggles.

Her way of putting me at ease is exactly what I need, after the stress I'm feeling after moving in with a total stranger. While Twiggy wasn't applying any pressure, I still think that I might have to watch my step or possibly be faced with a premature eviction.

The conversation pauses as we scan the vast menu and though everything sounds delicious, the waiter makes a few helpful suggestions, making the decisions easier.

"How're things at your new place? Getting along okay with...wha t's his name again?" she asks politely.

"He likes to be called Twiggy. That name wasn't familiar to me until I checked Wikipedia," I laugh.

"Twiggy! He must be thin as a rail!"

"Yeah, he's slender. And not just his waistline. He's got a slender little stick, too."

"You already went there, huh? That didn't take long."

"Oh no, that hasn't happened and hopefully, it never will. But I have seen the pix!"

She laughs easily when talking about sex and I adore her for that. It's nice to be able to have a pleasant conversation, even with some sexual innuendoes included, with my new friend. I don't always get along that well with straight women, and this is a welcome change.

The food begins to arrive, and as the fragrant aroma of her lobster bisque reaches me, I'm a little sorry that I chose the stuffed mushroom caps for my appetizer, though they are delectable.

Throughout the lunch, I encourage Ruby to tell me all about her drag queen brother, Rudy aka Rubee Red Lips. At one point, she reaches into her Hermes bag, producing one of those old-fashioned photo albums, filled with old photos of Rubee in her costumes. Some of the pix are even in black and white!

"She really did like to highlight her lips, didn't she?" I ask, noting that Rubee always wore very bright, very red lipstick. Of course, what else would a Queen named Rubee Red Lips wear?

"And she loved that red sparkle dress," Ruby replies, pointing out that the same costume was worn at many different events. "It was different in those days. Simpler. More campy than most shows today. Rubee loved to dress up and sing in front of a crowd at a club. But there wasn't much more to it than that, although the club boys did love her. Especially when she closed the show with her Jungle Fever act."

I remembered when Ruby told me on the train about the simulated sex during the show's final act. There were even a few somewhat faded photos of her at the end of her act, licking her fingers, holding a young guy with a fine ass over her knee, and then acting as if she was fingering the young thing.

I thought it made for a helluva fine closing number.

Speaking of closings, we were finishing dessert, and I was thinking of heading back to Twiggy's place.

"Do you have a little time? I'd like to take you to my favorite fabric shop and introduce you to the owner. His name's Janus and I think he'll enjoy meeting you, my dear."

"But of course. Even if I had other plans, I'll always make time for you," I tell her.

STORY HOUR

Meeting Ruby was a random, life-altering event for me. What if she had entered a different car on the train from Baltimore? What if she had taken a different seat, rather than settling in next to me? Did some unseen force guide her in my direction? I don't know, but for whatever reason, it was a blessing for me to have found this treasure of a woman.

Likewise, meeting Janus was life-changing—but not random. This was done under the direct supervision of Miss Ruby, though of course, it wasn't apparent at the time that this meeting would have profound consequences for my new life here in Philly.

We didn't stay at the fabric store for long. Introductions, handshakes, air kisses, and a brief tour of the premises from Janus, and then we were gone. But the groundwork had been laid. However, Ruby wasn't finished with me yet.

"One more stop, and then I'll let you go, sweetie," she assures me, as we climb into an Uber. After a short ride, we reach our destination, The Free Library of Philadelphia.

No, not the grand building on the Parkway. Instead, we're at a small branch library in South Philly. The bright red awning announces the location as the Queen Memorial Library.

How fitting! I thought. A library memorializing Queens!

The welcoming atmosphere is immediately apparent, with colorful posters, conversational areas with comfortable seating, and private areas for quiet reading or research.

Behind the front desk sits a slender man, wearing glasses and a warm smile.

"Jalen, I want you to meet my dear friend, Mr. Karlovich," Ruby tells me.

Standing and offering his hand, I'm struck by his height. Being 6 foot 3 myself, I guess he must be at least 6'6" or more.

"You can call me Bobby," he says in a voice so soft it's almost a whisper.

I wonder if he always speaks that way or if it's because we're in the library.

"Mr. Karlovich is the head librarian at this branch."

I wonder why she's being so formal, but it seems inappropriate to ask

"He's a pro at planning community events, which is why I wanted to introduce you," she continues.

Turning her eyes to the very slender man, who was leaning slightly forward to meet the gaze of the much shorter woman speaking to him, she asks, "I think Jalen here might be a good candidate for a Story Hour session. Her drag name is Pridezilla. How fabulous is that?"

Bobby looks at me with refreshed eyes, in a new light.

"I never would have guessed," he teases, taking my arm in his, guiding me to a reading area where the walls are decorated with clowns, balloons, dinosaurs, superheroes and rainbows.

"Do you know anything about children's literature? Or perhaps you have a favorite book suitable for kids around 4 or 5 years old?"

Now, this conversation is unexpected and outside of my usual topics of discussion, so I falter at first.

"Uhmmmm, a book for kids....let me think a minute," I stammer.

"Don't worry, I have plenty of books to recommend to you. But let me make one suggestion. Don't do a cold read. Just like any performance, be prepared. Do your homework. Think you're up to the task?"

Admittedly, I'm interested. Of course, I know about Drag Queen Story Hours, though this will be my debut performance at one.

"I think this sounds marvelous! But, can I ask a question?"

Not waiting for an answer, I continue.

"Is there any chance of trouble? Do people around here protest or anything like that? Not that I'm scared; I just want to be prepared, like you said."

"I'm glad you asked," Bobby replies. "It shows you're aware of the current climate for us. And of course, I can't promise anything, but we haven't had any problems in the past, and this will be our 5th Drag Queen Story Hour. The parents have been very supportive and the kids...well, the kids just adore the Queens."

Two weeks later, I arrive at the Queen Memorial Library, dressed in my street clothes, an hour before story time. By the time I emerge from the dressing area, I'm transformed into the Magnificent Pridezilla, looking like a Queen in full makeup, wearing a wig about a mile high, with a bright blue evening gown and matching three-inch platform pumps. Plenty of beautiful, matching accessories complete my look.

Watching all those little Black and Brown faces staring up at me fills me with a joy that I hadn't experienced before. Bobby had informed me that I'd be the first Black Queen to read at their Story Hour, so I wanted to be a good example, to show them that a Black Queen can be both intelligent, entertaining and beautiful.

Remembering my own Kindergarten and primary grade teachers reading to our class in Baltimore, I make sure to treat these young darlings with respect. "You gotta give respect to get respect" was a mantra at my old schools.

"Good morning, Ladies and Gentlemen!" I greet them, gesturing openness with my arms. "I'm your Drag Queen Story Teller today. You may call me by my name, Pridezilla."

"You mean Bridezilla," one of the kids says, surprising me just a bit.

"Ahhh, you are very intelligent, I see," I reply, admiring the knowledge of this young lady. "But no, my name is Pridezilla, because I take pride in who I am and I'm also big and strong like Godzilla.

"I'm pride of me too," a young boy calls out.

"Yes, be proud of your pride," I encourage him, allowing the error to go uncorrected. They're only 4 and 5 years old, so perfection isn't required or expected.

These kids are precious, I'm thinking.

"Before I begin reading this story, I want to know who you are. So everyone, please stand, and let's go around and say our names, and then sit when you're finished."

Everyone stands, including me. Their young eyes study me intensely, as I tower over them. But I have no wish to intimidate them—quite the opposite. I want them to experience only friendliness and kindness from me.

"I'm Pridezilla!" I say in a strong voice, modeling how I want them to present themselves.

The group of ten quickly do the same, giving their names before taking their seats on the carpeted area.

And then I began the story, reading "I am Perfectly Designed" by Karamo Brown, a beautifully-written story about self-acceptance and found family.

When I finish, I asked if there are any questions.

"Am I perfectly designed?" is the first question, coming from Syreeta, the girl who had called me Bridezilla.

"You most certainly are. Can you tell me one thing about you that's perfect?" I ask.

"My hair. I love my hair," she answers without hesitation.

I'm smiling as a boy named Enrique asks, "Can I touch your hair, Pridezulla?"

I don't mind that he doesn't get my name exactly right. There are times when mistakes should be corrected, but this is not one of those times, I decide.

"Of course, come on up. Do you like the color?" I ask him, as he nods, touching my hair gently, then returning to his seat. "Her hair is so soft," I hear him whisper to the boy sitting next to him.

Kevin raises his hand politely, asking, "Can I go to the bathroom?"

I already know that the answer to this question is always "Yes, but take a bathroom buddy." One can never be too cautious when allowing children out of your sight.

Each child has a chance to speak. Some of them describe something they like about themselves; others asked questions about me. What I remember the most is that these children are aware, curious, expressive and polite.

Perhaps the most intriguing question is asked by Syreeta, who says, "Are you perfectly designed? That's a lot of makeup I see."

Luckily, I had anticipated that someone might ask a question like that, so I'm able to answer without missing a beat.

"Yes, I am perfectly designed. But I also like to change my design sometimes. Just like all of us change our clothes, you know? I have fun making even more designs for myself."

Syreeta seems satisfied with my answer, with no follow-up questions.

Then I introduce the second book that I'll read today, "Julián is a Mermaid" by Jessica Love. In this story, Julián tells his abuela (grandmother) that he wants to be a mermaid, and he later dresses up as one.

To prepare for this reading, I watched some experts in children's literacy read the book on YouTube, admiring how they described the action in the gorgeous illustrations, done by the author herself. I use a similar technique while reading the book to the young audience seated before me, describing Julián's vivid imagination.

Again, after the reading, I provide time for the children to react and ask questions, before they scatter to make their choices for books to take home with them that day.

As I'm talking with Bobby, expressing how much fun I had during Story Hour, Syreeta comes skipping up to us, holding her mother's hand.

"Mommy, this is Pridezilla. You saw her read to us, right?"

"I'm sorry if Syreeta was a little outspoken. She likes to say what's on her mind," her Mom says.

"Not at all! I love how she expresses herself. She's a lovely child! And I adore the way she dresses, with her matching buttons and bows. I know she learned that from you, Mama," I reply.

"Did you have fun today? Learn anything from the books?" her mother asks.

Scrunching her face for just a second, Syreeta thinks about her answer.

"I'm perfectly designed!" she exclaims proudly. "And...and...boys can be mermaids if they want to be."

I couldn't have answered the question better myself.

"Will you come back and read to us again sometime?" Syreeta asks. "I love you!"

She hugs me and my heart fills with joy as my eyes begin to water.

Up to this point, this was my favorite drag moment ever.

WHO'S THAT CHICA?

A fter waiting all day to hear back from Janus, he finally replies to my text.

●●●○○ Sprint LTE   7:03 PM   46% ■□

❮ Messages **King Janus**   Details

Congrats on your drag name. It suits you well. No time in the lineup for this week, but in two weeks, you can open the show. You'll be on with Ritzy Quackers and Midge. Prepare one song.

My heart skips a beat reading his message. Opening the show, well, I know that's the spot for a beginner like me. Ritzy Quackers? I don't know her personally, though I've seen her with the Snark Sharks. So, she's no amateur.

But Midge? She's an icon in the Philly drag world. Having her on the bill will guarantee a full house! Oh my god! Oh my god! Oh my god!

I cannot wait for these two weeks to go by. I have so much to do to get ready!

"Cobra, come here, wait till you hear about this!"

But Cobra isn't home to hear my good news. That'll have to wait until some other time..

Breakfast is the only staple in our house, the only time we share on a regular basis. Not because of anything I do. It's Lito...Cobra...who makes the effort, trying to find something like the traditional family time. Being the older one, that should be my responsibility. Sometimes, I feel guilty that I'm not more motherly.

I'm already getting used to calling him Cobra. I like that new name he chose for himself.

I think it would be a good thing to start a new tradition, where everybody selects a name for themselves early in life. You know, before things get too set in stone. How many of us have names we don't like, but we keep them for no apparent reason? My guess is there are millions of people in that situation.

As I start to prepare the coffee, Cobra comes in, shushing me away and taking over his usual duties.

"Just cornflay today! You heard? All we got is cornflay today, Mister Mister!"

That sets me off laughing.

"You remember when Tia Jacinta came to visit Mami from Puerto Rico? No matter what kind of cereal we was eatin', she always called it cornflay."

"I remember," I assure my brother. "She was too funny with her Rican ways. But she did try to help Mami out, and that was good."

"Eat your cornflay, bro," Cobra says, shaking the contents from a package of Froot Loops into my bowl. And don't be too frooty today," he jokes.

"You know I got a million things to do. In two weeks, I'm finally doing my first show at the club. You're gonna help me with sewin' up the costume, right?"

I already know the answer. I just want to hear him say it.

"I got you, Donnie. No worries! We gonna make you shine bright like a diamond!"

Today, I'm scheduled for both the lunch and dinner shifts at Rico, the only upscale Puerto Rican restaurant along Philly's unofficial "Restaurant Row," running along 13th Street from Walnut to Lombard. Our specialties are authentic Rican dishes, but at prices set to match those of our neighboring restaurants, drawing in the city's elite and powerful. Authenticity doesn't come cheap in this part of the city.

To be honest, we don't get a lot of authentic Ricans dining here. They're more likely to get their authentic Rican dishes up in the hood...Kensington. The food up there, where I live, is authentic and cheap. The best combination.

I'm very good at my job. I serve my customers with class, but I also throw in a little flair. You know, an extra twist of the hips, a wink and a nod, using my hands to accentuate my speech. And though the menu is printed in Spanish with English subtitles, it isn't necessary to speak fluent Spanish here. Lucky for me, since Mami raised us to speak English as our primary language.

Serving a table of four wealthy gentlemen, I turn on the charm. How do I know they're wealthy? Their watches. Dead giveaway every time. Not that they were trying to hide their upper-class positions, but if they were, I know that these types would never give up those status symbols wrapped around their wrists.

They're young, and I figure they're probably lawyers, who either work at nearby City Hall or at one of the prestigious law firms at Penn Center. One of them, in particular, catches my eye.

"What time do you get off, *chica*?" he asks me at one point during their meal. His companions laugh so loudly that the entire restaurant takes notice. His friends consider it a sign of disrespect, calling me a girl, but I think differently. I take it as a sign of interest.

"Working a double today," I answer, trying to be nonchalant. But I know my face is turning red as I look directly into his warm, brown, liquid eyes.

"I'll be back here at closing. See you then."

His friends continue to enjoy their meal, laughing as their conversation turns to different subjects. None of the others have any interest in someone they see as a servant, someone to be ignored except while placing an order for food.

On a weeknight, even a spot as popular as Rico is mostly deserted by the 9:30 PM closing time. I'm usually able to leave shortly after closing, as the busboys and kitchen staff would be involved in the clean-up activities. Waiters are exempt from that work.

I hadn't forgotten about my supposed "date" for the end of the shift. As a matter of fact, the thought of him had kept me preoccupied ever since I watched his fine ass go out the door with his buddies. Did I let out a small gasp when he turned and winked at me as he left? Ohh, my fluttering heart!

I'm used to disappointment when it comes to men. Most of the guys I meet are, well, let's say not the highest quality. A politician might describe them as "not the very best," and it would be difficult for me to argue with that assessment. Is it always going to be like that? Might I possibly meet a man who would appreciate me, who would respect me, who might actually...dare I say it...love me?

Just as I start to walk to the El for the ride home, there he is, standing two doors from the restaurant, looking fine as fuck, casually leaning against the wall, smoking a cigarette. *Oh well, no one's perfect*, is all I can say about that.

He doesn't move, waiting for me to approach him. I'm not about to pass up this opportunity, so I walk up to him, smiling nervously, extending my hand in greeting.

"You are one hella fine *chica*," he greets me.

"And you're one fine *chico*," I reply.

The smile disappears from his face.

"Make no mistake, *chica*, I am nobody's *chico*. You might as well learn that right now. If it's a boy you're looking for, then you got the wrong one. This is a man, a real man, you got standing here in front of you. If that's what you like, what you need, then maybe we can click. But if you're looking for some sissy boy, you better know right now that ain't me."

I admire self-confidence. I also admire strength and masculinity. I have no problem with his approach, even this soon in our...what? Our relationship? I'm really getting ahead of myself with thoughts like that.

"I'm Donnie." I introduce myself, not shying away from his macho introduction.

"Donnie, huh? I guess that'll do for now. Till I name you properly. But that can wait. I'm Mateo. And I think you're just about the prettiest gurl I ever laid eyes on."

I look at him silently, already planning the wedding and reception. Thinking about the size of my engagement ring, like a silly, white schoolgirl. Things like that don't happen in real life to hood gurls like me. Or do they?

"Let's go over to Club 18 for a drink and some talk. I like to watch them girlies dancing up on the stage while I relax. And I'll be honest, 'cause that's my style, I wanna get to know about you."

I'm hypnotized by everything about him. The voice, so deep, so *varonil*. His eyes, dark brown and yet so bright that they reflected the light around him. Tall, broad-shouldered, slim-waisted, and dressed to impress. Thick, black, wavy hair, atop a face of chiseled beauty, with every feature perfectly proportioned.

And of course, I know Club 18. The "girlies" he referred to are scantily-clad gogo boys. Some of them are femme, dressing in panties, stockings, garters, and the like, while others perform their boylesque routines, dressed in jocks, briefs, or thongs.

"Of course, Mateo," I answer, using my breathiest voice, contrasting my feminine side with his clear display of masculinity.

Inside the club, one of the "girlies" spots him instantly, rushing over to greet him, taking hold of his arm and guiding him to what I presumed was his usual table. The girlie acted as if I were invisible.

On the other hand, I study her closely, seeing every detail in her outfit of red thong panties covered with a black fishnet minidress. Her shoulders strike me as just a little too broad and her Adam's Apple protrudes just a bit too much for my tastes. However, I recognize competition when I see one, and she might be a potential problem. I think Mateo brought me here on purpose, so I can see exactly the type of "women" that he likes.

"Bourbon for me and a Cosmo for my lady here." With that command, he waves my competitor away, pulling back the chair for me like a proper gentleman.

Classy! I think. *And, he called me "his" lady.*

Leaning back into his chair, facing the stage where the boylesque show was going strong, his eyes widen with interest.

As if by magic, a $20 bill was in his hand.

"Pick your favorite and tip her with this. I want to see which one you like."

I study the group of five beautiful young men, all gyrating to the music, and caught the eye of a handsome, muscular dancer with very dark Black skin and bedroom eyes. He was not only the most masculine of the group, dressed in a leather thong and harness, but also the one with the best body, abs clearly showing as he thrusts his groin against a pole.

I wave the 20 in his direction, and he immediately comes over to our table, smiling at Mateo, then taking a quick glance at me, as he then turns and faces away, his ass bouncing to the music, waiting for me to place the tip wherever I want. I push my hand against his waist, signaling for him to turn, and then reached deep inside the pouch of his thong, leaving the bill nestled against his dick.

"Nice move," Mateo says approvingly, as the dancer returns to the stage. "Feel anything you like in there?"

In reply, I smile and lick my lips, then pucker up and send an air kiss over to the dancer.

Mateo laughs. "I like your style. I like it a lot. But you know what I really like about you?"

"What is it, sugar? My hips? My sexy body?" I start rubbing my hands suggestively over myself, craving attention, not wanting him to enjoy the dancing bois and gurls too much.

"No, what attracted me right away is your face. My god, you could be a model and you'd be the most beautiful gurl on the runway."

Who wouldn't be thrilled with a compliment like that?

"I'm gonna start performing. My first drag show is coming up soon. You like drag queens, right?" I ask hopefully.

"Condragulations, my dear!"

As soon as he said that, I know he's a fan, using a line straight out of RuPaul's *Drag Race*.

"I have a challenge for you. I hope you'll accept it. Have you ever tried to pass as a female? Like, do the makeup in a way that isn't an exaggeration, but a more natural look?"

"Can't say I ever tried that, no. Why do you ask?"

"I'm attending a high-profile event in a few days. I'd like to take you as my date, but I want you to look as naturally feminine as you can achieve."

"Why? Are you worried about being with this type of gurl? The type that I am?"

A pained expression comes over his face.

"Not at all! I have confidence in who I am and in what I like. And if anyone there recognizes that you're not a natural female, that's okay by me. I just want to see if you can handle this challenge. And I also want to see the reactions of certain people when they see you."

"What kinda event is this?" I ask, not certain if I should accept his challenge or not.

"You ever heard of Díner en Blanc?"

Of course. I might live in the hood, but I'm not isolated in a cave.

I keep those thoughts to myself, outwardly nodding and smiling.

"I never thought I'd ever get a chance to attend an event like that. I mean, the elegance of it all, with hundreds, or is it thousands of fancy guests all dressed to impress in their best white outfits."

My words come spilling out of my mouth so fast, I have to stop for a gulp of air.

"Then you do know. It's an occasion that demands etiquette and decorum. And it can get you attention. Lots of attention. From people who I think might really appreciate your unique beauty."

Inside, I'm dying with anticipation.

"I want you to look and act as glamorous as possible. After all, you'll be with one of the hottest men on the planet, if I do say so myself."

He has no lack of self-confidence, but he isn't being cocky, because everything he's saying is true.

"Tell me what I have to do. And when is it?"

"It's next Wednesday night. You know they keep the location secret till the last minute. And it's fun, a lot of fun. I've been there the last three years and always have a great time. But this year, I'd like to have a very special lady at my table, seated with me, and I want us both to make a splash with the crowd. You in?"

"Honey, you don't even know. I'm gonna spend all day tomorrow watching female makeup videos on YouTube. I'm definitely up for this!"

After spending more time talking about our plans for the event, and getting to know each other better, Mateo calls for an Uber and directs the driver to take me home. Just before I get into the car, he takes me by the waist, giving me a long, hard kiss good night, right there at the curb.

There's no demand for sex that first night. I think that's a good sign, right?

NO ROMANCE

After the Drag Queen Story Hour at Queen Memorial Library, I felt the joy from the kids and their parents. Wanting to hold on to that feeling, and not wanting to go right back home, I take a walking tour to get better acquainted with my new city, Philadelphia. Dressed in my street clothes, I take a bus to the area they call Center City and walk rather aimlessly, finding the sites quite charming.

Eventually though, it's time to return home. Ever since my arrival, it seems that every interaction with Twiggy ends up going in the wrong direction. There's a lack of understanding, of trust, of appreciation for each other. I have a vague feeling of being uncomfortable every time I'm in the house and I'm already thinking of looking for a different living situation.

Twiggy has been drinking heavily, greeting me with a slurred, "Good to see you, honey bunny," as soon as I cross the threshold. Pretending not to notice, I try to make a quick exit for my room, but Twiggy would have none of that.

"Here, sit right here, my darling," he insists, patting the cushion next to him on the sofa.

Trying not to be rude, since I'm well aware that he had opened his home to a stranger, I ease myself onto the couch, crossing my arms and holding my knees—a defensive posture, for sure.

"Have I told you yet just how much I adore your style?" he asks, reaching for my wrists and moving my hands from my knees into his sweaty palms, caressing my hands with his fingers.

Suddenly, he lunges for my mouth with his, pressing his lips harshly against mine, forcing my mouth open with his probing tongue.

My mind races with a rush of emotions. I wasn't expecting this and hadn't prepared myself for this sudden, rapid advance.

My first inclination is to just comply. I mean, it isn't like I never had sex with a man without being physically attracted to him. In this lifestyle, one has to sometimes make the best of less-than-inviting circumstances.

This little man is now on top of me, humping like a dog against my unaroused privates, reaching for the waist of his pants to free himself of the constraints.

"Hold on, hold on there, what do you think you're doing?" I finally blurt out, pushing his lightweight body off of me.

As he falls back onto the cushions of the sofa, he proceeds as if he hasn't heard a word I'd said, opening his pants, pulling out his small, pink dick and stroking himself hard and fast. He climaxes in about 5 seconds, his milkiness dripping down the few inches of his still-throbbing dick.

As soon as he finishes, his mood changes to one of fury. Sitting bolt upright, he looks at me with disdain and proclaims, "Look what you made me do; look at this mess! I was saving this to make a deposit in your pussy, and now it's all just wasted."

How pathetic, I think. *Where did he ever get such an idea? Just because I'm a drag queen doesn't automatically make me a total bottom slut.*

I was just about to get up and leave the room without a word, when he steals my move, abruptly going into his bedroom and slamming the door shut.

I'm left wondering what's going to happen next between us. Am I about to be evicted before I had even settled in?

Less than an hour later, my phone buzzes with a text notification, awakening me from a light, yet fitful sleep.

"Hello and I hope you won't mind this message. Can we meet for lunch tomorrow? I'm interested in getting to know you. And just to be clear, yes, I am asking you out on a date."

It was from Bobby, the librarian.

"I'd love to go on a date with you," was my quick reply.

After I serve us both breakfast, I go to school—most days, anyway. And then, after school, since Donnie's usually at work, I like to go over to Liphe's house. He's the one who did my cobra tatt. But it isn't Liphe who's captured my young heart. It's his little brother, Navarro, aka Navi.

We play video games—for hours and hours. We switch between Final Fantasy VII Rebirth, Dragon's Dogma II, and Star Wars Outlaws.

Today, we're playing Fortnite, but I'm losing my concentration because Navi is sitting so close, his eyes narrowing as he focuses on the screen, and his legs spread invitingly wide.

"You know," he starts, never moving his eyes from the screen, "I ain't gonna wait forever. You're 14 and next year you'll be a sophomore. How many virgin boys you think our school got in the sophomore class?"

He's right. We both know it. For some reason, I've been holding back, refusing his advances except for our hot makeout sessions. I love when he's tongue-kissing me, but I get scared when he tries to get past second base. I get excited when he plays with my nipples, but as soon as he starts reaching into my pants, I freeze up.

"I don't know why you think you're so fuckin' special," he continues. "It ain't like I lack experience. Since I'm in the sophomore class, it's my duty to show you little freshmen how it gets done. And I do a proper job of it. You can ask around."

"Plus, it's your duty to relieve me of my tension. I do got needs," he adds.

I already know. The boys at school talk. We all talk about sex, all the time. Most talk about which girls are easy and which ones won't put out. But my crew, though we keep it on the low, we talk about the older guys and which ones like boys, and how it all goes down.

"I'm gonna be the one that breaks you open. Yeah, I'm gonna pop you good. You already know that, right? You give your pussy to any of the other guys in my class, I'll fuckin' kill ya. You do understand that, right?"

I lose all concentration on the game. Instead, my eyes are drawn to the big bulge I can see in Navi's pants, and I do want it. I want it so, so bad.

"Not only take your pussy first, but you gonna get my initials in the middle of your tramp stamp. You know I already got my mark on the asses of more than a couple bitches. It don't mean we're married. It just means I was the first to crack their ass wide open. And you gonna wear my mark, and wear it proudly, ya heard? My brother'll do the tatt, but I'm gonna be there watchin'."

"Soon, Navi. I promise. I'm gonna take the dick soon. I just gotta prepare some, that's all."

"What's to prepare? You bend over, I give you some spit and I start my invasion. It'll be over fast. And you're gonna love it. I bet you'll be back for my dick over and over after you get it that first time."

Just hearing him talk about it, how he has it all planned out already, has me breathing hard, as he bends in my direction, forcing my mouth open with his tongue, reaching inside my shirt and squeezing my hard little nips.

I just wish he'd be a little more romantic. His way sounds so sterile, soulless, empty. What if I told Navi I wanted it to be like the setting in one of those romance novels? You know, a beautiful hotel room, a bathtub surrounded by scented candles, rose petals all around the place? I could dress in some fancy shmancy outfit and he could wear one of those thick hotel bathrobes. He could be my Romeo and I would be his Juliet...

I almost open my mouth to share my fantasy romance with him, when he whispers, "Yeah, you're gonna love it when I'm bustin' you open and bustin' my nutt inside ya."

Letting out a heavy sigh, I whisper back, "Yes, babe, I'm sure I'm gonna just love it."

I think it's gonna go down just like Navi described it. No romance for me. Maybe I don't deserve it.

WHO'S A
JACKOFF?

A s each day begins anew, my sense of familiarity conflicts with my sense of being in uncharted waters. The familiar is comforting, such as Lito, I mean, Cobra, fixing breakfast each morning and making jokes as we keep tabs on each other.

The new and exciting aspects of my life present themselves as challenges and opportunities. My first show is my highest priority, requiring my full concentration. But now, an unexpected wrinkle appears in the shape of Mateo and the opportunity to attend a world-class event, Díner en Blanc.

"Apple Jack-offs is on the menu this beautiful morning," Cobra greets me as I stand at the kitchen entrance. "They had a special at the Dollar Store, so I stocked up for us. That means you gonna be eating Jack-offs every day this week, ya heard?"

"Just make sure to serve cow's milk with the cereal and real cream in the coffee. No substitutions please, *cabron*!" I joke.

"Learn anything in school yesterday?" I then ask, playing my pseudo-parental role.

"Yeah, I did learn something useful for once. Teacher told us that Juliet was 13 years old when she hooked up with her man, Romeo. And guess what, I'm already 14."

Hearing his sigh, I know where this is heading.

"Wanna talk about it?"

He sighs again.

"Well, Navi told me the guys in his class are calling me the Virgin Mary, and one boy even called me the Virgin Fairy. And they're all laughing behind my back 'cause I ain't give it up yet."

"Ohhhh, I see. And that bothers you?"

"Course it bothers me. You think I want them boys referring to me as the Virgin Mary? I hate that. And Navi keeps on tellin' me that it's time for me to get my tramp stamp and that the initials inside better be his, or he's gonna kill me."

"Do you like Navi?"

"Sure, I do. But he talks about that first fuck like it ain't nothing. Like he don't even try to be romantic about it or nothin'. Am I wrong to want something nice for that first time?"

"No, you're not wrong," I assure my little brother. "Did you say anything to Navi about that?"

"No, you think I should tell him I want him to be romantic with me?"

"I can't give much advice here. You already know what happened to me. I got my tramp stamp when I was younger than you, and you've seen the initials there. J.R. for Johnny Reyes. Yeah, he used me that first time, and there was no romance involved. Used me, got me tatted up like I belonged to him, and then he went off and hit Whitey's ass. That's why me and him got the exact same stamp. Mister Johnny Reyes had his fun with both of our asses on the very same night. My first time gettin' dick was the last time I ever seen Johnny's. So, the best I can tell you is, make the best decision for what you want. You understand?"

"Yeah, I got you," Cobra replies. "Maybe I'll say something to Navi about it. But I can't wait much longer. There's no way I'm gonna stay bein' the Virgin Mary of my class."

Changing subjects, I tell my little bro about the invitation to Díner en Blanc, and the requirement to look as feminine as possible.

"First, let me check on the dinner. Ain't never heard of that one before," he tells me, checking his phone for information.

"Wow, that's one impressive party. Damn, everybody's all in white. I'm lucky it still came up for me. I was spellin' dinner with two Ns."

"Mateo doesn't want Drag Queen style makeup like we're gonna do for the show, so I was thinking we could watch female makeup videos for ideas. You know, models, of the female variety."

We giggle while Cobra begins searching.

"I don't know. Is this what you're looking for? Seems bland to me, but maybe that'll work."

I looked over at his phone, watching a pale blonde model applying a very subtle shade of foundation.

"Not that subtle. Too boring. It's gotta stand out, but not shout out. You got me?"

"Hmmmm, maybe we're taking the wrong approach. Maybe there's someone who got that look just right. Let me check."

I hear a familiar song and I know instantly what he's looking at. Troye Sivan performing in his video for "One of Your Girls."

"You're a genius!" That's the exact look I want. The face makeup is perfection. Look at the subtle white shading near the eyes, the soft pink lipstick, the arch of the brows. I think we can do that, right?"

"Damn straight we can," Cobra replies.

"And I'm inspired by his white outfit, too. Of course, I can't be showing the crotch like that, but the sheer slip dress, with the bodysuit underneath showing, that's cool. Just a longer version, I think."

"And the lacey sleeves, oh my, that screams feminine elegance, and that's the very look for you!" Cobra is clearly excited about the possibilities and I'm feeling it, too.

"We need a whole new makeup set, though. We don't have anything even close to those shades. And we have to remember the white nail polish too!"

One challenge has been easily overcome with the help of my brother. The basic idea for the dinner outfit was decided on that quickly. I can count on Cobra to do the shopping, if I don't have time to do it myself, because I have to work on the choreography for the show, which is coming up fast.

VIRGINITY

"Today's my day off, so I don't have to rush back to work. Maybe we can spend the afternoon together."

That's the text I get from Bobby right before we're scheduled to meet.

Lunch is both delicious and pleasant. Bobby's charming, quite the opposite of Twiggy. And funny, too. Being a librarian, he's also an amazing source of knowledge.

"Your nickname should be Google," I tease him.

"You want to do something silly with me today?"

His soft, melodic voice is music to my ears "How silly is silly?" I ask.

"When I was a kid, I always loved amusement parks. The rides. The fun. Playing those dumb games of chance where you never win a prize. Did you like those parks?"

"You're talking to Mister Roller Coaster right here!" I tell him. I always had so much fun at Ocean City; the Looping Star is the best ride ever."

"Then let's do something spontaneous. Wanna go to a park with me? I get tired of the same routine all the time. Unless you already have other plans."

"No, let's do it. Sounds like fun and I sure could use some of that right about now. You wanna take a bus or the train? I don't know what's best."

"No, Sugar. We'll take my car. And instead of heading for the shore, let's go west and I'll take you to Hershey Park. They have rides, a zoo, and of course, a chocolate factory. Just like Willie Wonka...well, almost."

Bobby makes me feel comfortable throughout the day. Just acting like silly kids at the park sounded like an ideal way to spend an afternoon. During the drive to Hershey, Bobby blasts his playlist of old school soul classics.

His mix includes "Respect" by Aretha Franklin, "Let's Stay Together" by Al Green, and "Living for the City" by Stevie Wonder.

Other artists:

The Four Tops

Diana Ross and the Supremes

Patti LaBelle

Ray Charles

Marvin Gaye

Luther Vandross

Roberta Flack

Nina Simone

Smokey Robinson

Teddy Pendergrass

Barry White

Tina Turner

And more!

Before I know it, we're pulling into the huge parking area for Hershey Park.

We share a love for roller coasters and this park boasts several, including an old-style wooden coaster called The Comet. I could have ridden that one all day, but Bobby had other favorites that he was eager to share with me. including the Sooper Dooper Looper, Wildcat's Revenge and Skyrush. And those were just the roller coasters!

We spent the day riding, without spending hours standing in line, since this cloudy weekday kept some visitors away.

As dusk approaches, we relax by a stream that flows through the park. Sitting on a bench, watching as groups of ducks glide over the gentle rush of the carp-filled waters, he puts his arm around me, holding me close.

"May I?" he asks, moving his face towards mine.

"Yes," is my simple reply, feeling his lips brushing mine, then lingering for a deep, full kiss.

It's a magical moment, forever etched into my memory.

He sits back against the bench rest, comfortable with a moment of silence after a day of screaming as we roared down the inclines of the coasters.

"Hey, you! What the fuck you think you're doing, out here in public, acting like that?"

The words shatter our peaceful moment.

Some random guy, red-faced with anger, is approaching us in a threatening manner.

I don't even have time to react, but Bobby shows no signs of hesitation, grabbing his phone and recording the encounter.

"What are we doing? We're two gay men, enjoying a peaceful time here at the park. And I'm warning you right now, take one more step and this video will be viral before you even get home. Are you prepared to lose your job, your reputation, for harassing us when we haven't done anything wrong?"

That stops the man in his tracks as he considers what might happen if he's seen on video attacking us. Backing down from the challenge, he hides his face with his hands, backing away, but unable to resist getting in one final insult. "You fuckin' faggots think you own the place. You're gonna find out someday. Believe me, you are gonna find out!"

As quickly as he had come upon us, he disappears over a small hill.

My heart is racing. It isn't new for me to be confronted like that, but I had let my guard down, and this man had shaken me. Bobby drew me closer, feeling my body trembling, and he simply holds me, comforting me.

"If I ever get the chance, I will always protect you. That's my promise to you," he states firmly.

The ride back to Philly is quiet, with a soft jazz playlist providing a background for my thoughts. I was reflecting on the events of the day, frankly surprised that this man, whose first impression was that of a meek, gentle lover of books and academia turned out to be someone much more deep, stronger, and more assertive than I had imagined.

Heading east on the Schuylkill Expressway, nearing the exits for Center City, Bobby says, "I can drive you to your place, or, if you want,

I could take the next exit and we could go to my place. Your decision, but I need to know whether to take this next exit or not."

"Your place works for me. Go ahead, take the next exit."

I'm confident that this is the right decision.

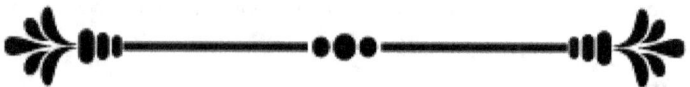

Once again, Cobra, my little bro, isn't in the kitchen making breakfast this morning. Unusual, but not unheard-of, so I'm not alarmed. I put on the coffee, pour myself a bowl of "cornflay" and try to prioritize what I need to get done today.

It's Friday night, so I want to watch the show at Fuego, and try to get backstage to talk with the Queens performing tonight, looking for advice before my first show. Wednesday is the big dinner with Mateo. And then two days later, I have to be ready with my act.

The front door opens and Cobra comes rushing in, grabbing a coffee and sitting gingerly across from me.

"Listen, I'm sorry if I didn't give you any great advice yesterday. Part of me wants to joke around about you giving up your virginity, and maybe it came across like I wasn't really hearing your concerns. So, no jokes about being a Virgin Mary from me, I promise."

"You ain't gotta worry about that anyways. What's done is done," he answers, then stands up and turns around, lifting the back of his shirt. And there it is. The tramp stamp. The initials "NR" for Navarro Rivera are etched in the middle of an intricate design. My first thought is that it's a beautiful tattoo. But of course, I'm aware of the implications.

"You wanna talk about it? It looks great; I'll say that much."

"Well, I didn't get no romantic evening, no hotel room, no roses or flowers or nothin'. But I figured this is how it's gonna be for me. I guess I'm just a cunt for the boys at school to use. For now, but maybe not forever."

I don't want to sound judgmental in any way, so I decide to let Cobra do most of the talking. After all, this was his decision, his life.

"Anything else?" I encourage him to continue. "Did he use protection?"

I can't help myself. I have to know if I need to tell my brother about the importance of safer sex practices.

"Yeah, he wore a condom. At least, I'm pretty sure he did. I know he put one on to start. And then, it was just how he told me it was gonna be. He bent me over the back of a chair, used a little spit and invaded me."

"Just like that?"

"Yep, exactly like that. He ain't even said nothin' to me. I thought maybe he'd whisper in my ear or somethin', but no, just a couple grunts, a couple deep pushes inside me and the next thing I know, he's already pullin' outta me and puttin' his junk away."

"He hurt you much?"

"Maybe a little, but he was done right quick. And there was nothing really special about it, either."

"But he let you sleep over there? In his bed? 'Cause you just now came home."

"Nah, I didn't get to stay over. His brother did the tatt and that took some time. They said it was important to get my stamp on me

95

the same night I gave up the cherry. But once that was done, I came back home."

Cobra saw my questioning look.

"Ok, I was outside havin' me a smoke. My nerves was a little on edge, so I got me...I got us a pack, ok?"

He tosses the green pack of Newports on the table. I grab one out of the pack and light up, inhaling deeply. That feels so good.

We both swore we were done with cigarettes, but somehow, we always find excuses to go back to the habit. Today, we told ourselves we could even smoke in the house, seeing as how it was Cobra's "Losing My Virginity" Day.

"You sure you're gonna be okay? I gotta go see Whitey about all the shit I'll be doin' this week. You gonna go into school?"

"Damn straight I'm goin' to school. You think I ain't wanna show off my stamp? I'll show them I ain't the Holy Fuckin' Virgin Mary no more!"

"Hey, before I go, you want any S'mores?" Cobra asks me, teasing me about how it was before I found my name.

"Git goin', young virgin!" I holler after him, as he heads out the door. Two can play that game.

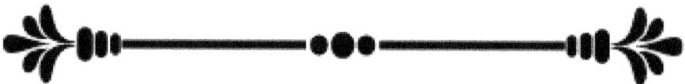

On my way to Whitey's, my usual routine, crossing Madison Street, making the Sign of the Cross at the sight of Jamal's kicks, forever dangling from the overhead wire. I came prepared, in case my little red friend might still be in the area, so I scatter a few sunflower seeds, just as I hear him chirping at me.

"C'mon over here, little guy," I whisper. "I ain't gonna hurt ya. Look what I got for ya."

I hold a few seeds in my cupped hand, hoping that Rojo, as I named him, might fly onto my palm. But no such luck. Rojo takes a few seeds from the ground up to his mate, still in the nest on top of the pole, and stays there.

"Ok, I understand," I tell him. "You have a job to do. Protecting your lady and keeping an eye on them kicks up there. You do you, buddy," I tell him, winking and going on my way.

I wonder if Jamal is also watching me, guiding me, helping me to succeed in getting through all the obstacles this neighborhood places in front of us.

Some things ain't never gonna change, I think. *But that don't mean that everything gotta stay the same.*

Whitey is watching that Troye Sivan video again, noting every detail of the outfit.

"That choice of boots was bold," is the first thing he says when he sees me at the door.

"Yeah, I think I need something a little different for my feet. And I won't be wearing a dress that short."

"But before we get into the details of the outfit, I got a problem," I continue.

"What's that?"

"Well, you've been my best friend my entire life and now, all of a sudden, I feel like I don't even know what to call you. Am I just supposed to not say your name no more? I'm a little confused, to be honest. It seems weird to call you Whitey now. Maybe I can just call you 'Amiga'?"

"C'mon Donnie, don't be like that. We've been friends for too long. Besides, I got the answer to your problem, anyways."

"Tell Mami what's up. You gonna join our trend and change your name? It seems funny that we're all doing it, but it also feels like it's the right thing to do."

"Would you just shut up for one fuckin' minute so I can tell you?" The smile on his face showed that he wasn't really annoyed with me.

However, I did shut up to let him speak. Active listening mode activated.

"Last night, I was doing my OnlyFans show, and you know I use an identity on there."

"Yep, Bandana Boy. You know I watch you on there, but I won't tell you what I'm doing when I see you performin'."

We both laugh.

"And I say this all the time, but you should call yourself Banana Boy, 'cause you do got one helluva large banana you show off for your followers."

"Yeah, yeah, but you also know the real reason I wear a bandana. It's to hide this scar."

He didn't have to point to the 4-inch scar on the side of his neck. I was there when he got wounded. Whitey's father had cut him with a knife, trying to kill his own son, when he had caught me, another guy, and Whitey, all of us naked and hard and playing what we used to call our "boy games." Naked boy games.

"It ain't really look that bad," I try to assure him.

"You're right about that. Though every time I see it or think about it, my head is filled with horrible memories. You know that. But other dudes, when they see it, they ain't know how it happened. And they ain't gotta know nothin' about the back story. I found out some guys...no, a lot of guys...think it's sexy and they think it makes me even tougher than I really am."

"So what's this got to do with your name?"

"Don't you see? I gotta stop hidin' from my past. I gotta accept it. I wanna be...what's the word they use when they talk about being true to yourself?"

"Honest?" I asked.

"No, c'mon Donnie. I'm talkin' about being authentic. I was just watching a podcast with some Queer author on there, talkin' about trying to make his characters authentic, and that's a good thing to be."

I remain silent, not wanting to interrupt my friend.

"So last night, during my show, I was doing the thing with my banana, when the bandana slipped off my neck. My first thought was to cut the show short and get off camera. But right away a guy commented, 'Dude, that slash is sexy! Why you hiding it?' And then the comments started flooding the chat, and then the tips started coming in faster and bigger than ever!"

"Wow, not what you expected, huh?"

"Nope, not at all. But then I thought about it and decided those guys watching last night were right. I was too blinded by my hatred for that man to see that he left me with a mark that I just gotta live with. And it's a bonus that guys find it hot 'n' sexy. I guess I just never looked at it that way."

Whitey continues, "So Donnie, meet your old best friend who's also your new best friend. It's me, Slash. Whaddya think?"

This is part of what I love about being a part of a creative, Queer community. We can rise to the occasion; we can overcome obstacles; we can face adversity head-on; and we can be our authentic selves.

That's what I think.

I walk over and give my friend the tightest hug that I can.

I whisper into his ear, "I'm so proud of you. You didn't run away and hide. You let them see you. And look what happened. They love you for it. And guess what? I love you, too, Slash!"

"Damn, bish, you bringin' a tear to my eye with all that gurl talk," Slash says, but I know he's proud of himself.

I change the subject, so we don't get too emotional.

"Let's get to work and make the final decisions on my outfit. Next weekend will be here before you know it. And tell me what you really think about Troye's boots."

THE SHOW GOES ON

The Friday night drag shows at Fuego don't always include elaborate costumes or productions. During special occasions, such as appearances by Drag Stars like Melba Toasty and the Kop Tarts, the staff will make a special effort in their honor.

But frankly, it's different when the hometown Queens are on the bill. No one will draw the curtains open and closed for us. We have to pull the curtain to the side as we make our entrance, stage right, and then after our performance, we simply walk off, stage left.

I even saw a Queen stomp off the stage one night when the DJ made a mistake and started playing the wrong song instead of the one the Queen was prepared for. I mean, she could have tried to wing it, and maybe no one would have even noticed. Then again, she might not have wanted to be seen badly lip-syncing to some unfamiliar song. Or, she could have done what I would have, which would be to holler up at the DJ, "Damn, can you please at least play the correct fuckin' song?"

So, glitches can and do occur. I have to be prepared for anything because I'll be damned if my drag debut is going to be ruined by anyone...except possibly myself. If that happens, I'll own it, but I have plenty of confidence in my abilities.

My favorite spot to watch the shows is from the balcony, giving me a birds-eye view of everything. Tonight is no different as Janus the King introduces the opening act.

"Ladies, ladies, ladies and all you bitches, too! Please give me your attention. Thank you. Tonight, we have two of the top artists from right here in Philly. One of them we had to Drrrrraggggg in from the streets, but she has agreed to perform for us....as long as we Drrrrrrrag-gggg her back out at the end. Please give a warm welcome for The Lady Starr Kissed!"

She's looking good, I think, since there's no one close by to dish with. Shows sometimes bring out my snarky side, but not tonight. At least, not yet.

She's singing along to a track of Stockard Channing's rendition of "There Are Worse Things I Could Do," her solo as Rizzo in the movie *Grease*. A good song choice, as the crowd eats it up, rewarding her with plenty of tips.

She continues with other well-known songs from the same movie, and I note that her costume matches the film's 1950s vibe, with her poodle skirt swaying to show a fancy petticoat beneath, a short-sleeved angora sweater covering her huge boobs, and I have to smile at the sight of her bobby socks and saddle shoes.

Her set continues with two songs popularized by Olivia Newton-John from the same movie, first with a solo, "Hopelessly Devoted To You," and ending with a song that was done as a duet in the movie with John Travolta, "You're The One That I Want."

Lady Starr Kissed sings both roles, but I let out a shriek when I see that she had made arrangements with Eliud, that elusive, non-exclusive bartender, to join her on the stage as her dance partner. He's dressed like Travolta in that part of the movie: Tight black jeans, even tighter black tee shirt with rolled-up sleeves, black shoes and white socks. An unlit cigarette dangles lasciviously from his lips as he rocks his hips like a pro.

It's captivating. It's divine. What a show!

Even I toss a fiver down on the stage.

This Friday night at Fuego is smokin'!

I'm impressed with the show, noting the sense of continuity. I want to use that as a model for my show.

Naturally, not everyone thinks the same way, as the Snark Sharks move in for the kill.

Ru-Barb: "Will someone please toss that girl a lifesaver? I don't mean a life preserver. I'm talkin' about the candy. Cause gurl, I can smell the garlic from that pizza she ate before the show all the way down here in Row Number Five."

Nepharious: "Whew! I thought it was Abraham Lincoln, the Vampire Hunter, we were watching. I kept expecting her to pull a crucifix outta her bra to fight off the night creatures, but I guess she figured the garlic would do the trick!"

Ru-Barb: "I will admit, her act made me hungry. Wanna go get some Italian after the show? I love garlic sauce on my pasta!"

From the balcony, I make my way down to the stage, approaching where King Janus stands.

"You know the rules. No visitors backstage. Just performers and their assistants, if they have any."

"Uhmm, I just wanna talk to Lady Starr Kissed. I'd love to get some advice from her about my show for next week."

"Damn gurl, what part of No don't you understand?"

"But I just wanna..."

"I heard you the first time. Now you flat-out disrespecting me. You can talk to the lady. Just not here and not now. And next week, when you're back there, you'll be happy that I'll be out here making sure you're safe and have your privacy."

Of course, he's right.

"You think she might talk to me?"

"Gurl, how the hell would I know that? But I do know most performers leave out the back door right after they get outta their costumes. So maybe you might meet her back there. Or, take your chances in here, 'cause she also might stay in the club for a while. Some performers do that, too. I don't tell them what to do. They're grown and make their own decisions. Now step back, bitch. I got an introduction to do."

Not sure if I should head for the back door or stay in the club, I take into consideration that I don't want to miss the next performer. So I stay, but in the front of the crowd on the ground floor. That way, I might be able to see if Lady Starr Kissed goes out the back.

"Give it up once more for Lady Starr. She's a Starr, all right. Remember the name, Lady Starr Kissed. She's a treat, isn't she?"

The crowd of mostly gay men, crowded at the front of the stage, applaud, cheer, and whistle their approval.

As the crowd grows quiet, I hear a voice calling my name. "Donnie, up here! Come on up! Watch the show with me."

Lots of people turn to see who's hollering like that. I don't have to look; I already know. But I look anyway. It's Mateo. I never saw him at Fuego before, and no way was I letting anyone in this crowd of bitches make a move on my man. I probably look like the Flash, a blur, as I rush back up to the balcony.

I'm already nestled in his arms, rubbing my ass against his body, by the time Janus begins the next introduction.

"Ladies, get your engines ready because this next guest is gonna rev you up! If you're not careful, she might DRAG you off to the races! One of my favorite ladies, here she is, Miss Chevy Chaser!"

And so the show begins, enter, stage right.

I'm snug in Mateo's arms, my eyes mostly closed, but he's interested in the performances. "That's gonna be you down there next week, right? Damn, you're gonna knock it outta the park. I know you will!"

Having Mateo encouraging me is important. It lets me know that he's supportive of my passion, which is drag. I've been performing alone in my bedroom for years now and I'm about to take that next step, sharing my gift with the world.

Chevy Chaser is dressed in a white gown that's so rounded below her waist that it appears to me like she's bouncing on a gigantic baseball. And for some reason, she keeps her hands on her hips, without any movements to go with her song. It isn't required that she dance, but at least show a little life, a little spark of something to bring the crowd alive. On top of that, her slow ballad is falling flat, failing to give the audience what they want...which is entertainment. I know I can do better than she's doing tonight. I hope that she's capable of a better performance, too. Maybe this just wasn't her night. I'm determined to bring the crowd to its feet when it's my turn to perform.

The show ends, exit, stage left.

The DJ returns to playing dance hits and the crowd joins in on the fun.

The Snark Sharks have their razor-sharp teeth at the ready.

Ru-Barb: "And it's one, two, three strikes you're out!"

Nepharious: "What in the holy fuck was that bullshit? I thought with a name like Chevy Chaser she might at least give us something sleek, something fast, something classic. But noooooo!"

Ru-Barb: "Don't even tell me you think a Chevy is a classic, gurl. But I will say, I'd be happy to chase her all the way down to the dealership over on Broad Street."

Nepharious: "Better call a tow truck honey, 'cause that broke-down ole model Chevy ain't goin' nowhere."

"Fuck, I forgot I wanted to talk to Lady Starr Kissed. Can we go see if she's still somewhere around here?" I ask Mateo.

"Let's go," he replies. But she'd already left the club, and I missed my chance to get some advice from her.

I forget my disappointment when Mateo takes my hand, leads me onto the dance floor, and proceeds to seduce me there at the club, for all to see. I hope Eliud is watching. And Divinity, too. *They can have each other*, I think, as Mateo grinds his hips into me.

Mateo leaves the club and goes home without me, saying he had an early day tomorrow. I go home alone, somewhat dejected. Mateo showing up at the club had been a surprise and I was ready to party with him all night. I don't want to end up in the dreaded "friend" zone.

He does maintain contact with a steady stream of texts, WhatsApp chats, and FaceTimes, but we don't spend any time together physically until he picks me up for dinner on Wednesday.

DÍNER en BLANC

White limos aren't an everyday sight in my poor Kensington neighborhood, but they aren't unknown, either. In May and June, many parents hire limos for their graduating kids. This is especially true when families with a history of little to no formal education reach the end of the 8th Grade. For these parents, many realize that might be the last graduation their child will ever experience.

Though I did graduate from 8th Grade, there was no celebration for me. Mami explained that she just didn't have the money. We walked over to school for the ceremony and walked back home. No gift, no party. Tonight will be my first limo ride.

Ready to make the grand exit from our small house to the waiting limousine, I'm aware that my crew, consisting of Cobra and Slash, had transformed me by creating an illusion of feminine beauty.

"Cobie, you're a genius!" I tell my brother, when he reveals my look for the first time.

"It's Cobra, not Cobie," he whines to me, and I playfully slap his wrist.

"Don't talk back to your big sister," I admonish him, though he understands that I'm kidding. "Cobra, Cobie, no matter what I call you, just know I love you," I tell him, meaning every word.

Inspired by Troye Sivan's "One of Your Girls" video, we went beyond simply copying his look. Our debates about whether to wear long, flowing hair or a short, blonde bob were fierce. I chose the shorter cut, as it gives a more youthful, carefree vibe. The very blonde hair makes my brilliant green eyes gleam.

Cobra did most of the makeup, and Slash is responsible for the overall look, including my dress and all accessories. They kept in mind that the goal isn't to look like a fabulous Drag Queen. Rather, the intention is for me to be a beautiful, young woman.

Modest, natural-looking lashes, accentuated with white eyeliner, contrast with the gentle pink blush several shades lighter than my pink lipstick. My nails, painted white with a pink border, are squared, with gently rounded edges, and at a fashionably moderate length.

The dress itself is stunning, a white slip dress with the hem just above my knees. White lace arm warmers add to the air of feminine mystique, with a hint of bad-girl naughtiness. Around my shoulders, a dainty, feathery boa, made to move slightly in even the softest breeze, so my appearance would never look stagnant.

I opted against wearing boots, which Troye did for his ultra-feminine look. My legs are sexy, and I like to show them off, particularly at a special event. The challenge in selecting the right shoes and stockings, when white is required, is to avoid looking like Nurse Ratched from the waist down.

Texting with Mateo while planning my outfit, I was relieved to learn that shoes in metallic colors are perfectly acceptable. My wardrobe already included both silver and gold heels in various heights, so I chose a style in silver with a moderate 3-inch stiletto heel, to be worn with sheer pantyhose designed with a hint of glitter. This gurl loves to shine!

All accessories are in silver, including chains, bracelets, and earrings. Tastefully done, casually elegant. Understated glamour is the theme, with nothing to distract from the radiant beauty of my face. That's the feature I want on everyone's mind, the topic of their gossipy conversations.

A limo in our neighborhood signals a special occasion in someone's life, so neighbors pay notice as the luxury vehicle pulls up to the curb. I step outside as soon as I see it, doing my supermodel walk as perfectly as anyone appearing on a runway or red carpet.

Did I wear a tad too much of Beyoncé's signature scent, Angels' Share by KILIAN Paris? Perhaps, but I find it hypnotically sweet, and I'm serving supreme femme tonight. Besides, my drag sister, Harloweena, who manages the perfume department at Macy's, keeps me in good supply of all the samples they get. That way, I'm always at the top of the perfume game.

Reaching the halfway point of my sidewalk runway stroll, Mateo exits the limo and I pause for a moment to appreciate his masculine beauty. With his wavy locks, chiseled face, and perfectly-proportioned body, he could be a supermodel himself.

His attire consists of a crisp, white linen suit from Prada, with tiny pearls sewn into the collar. A white satin tee shirt that would cost me a week's salary is accessorized with three strands of pearls at his neck.

The pearl earrings in both ears are stunning. A pair of summer white shoes, sparkling with encased rhinestones, complete the look.

Cobra comes running out of the house with his phone. "Please, let me be the first with pix of the glam couple on Insta! This look is going viral tonight, no doubt!"

Cobie's excitement was contagious. I feel my adrenaline rising, a star about to be born.

Our goal is not only to be seen, but also to be part of this elegant community event, so we don't break any of the protocols, not wanting to be accused of staging a publicity stunt.

The entire evening was breathtaking, spectacular, and in honor of its French origins, *magnifique*!

This "chic picnic" brings people from diverse backgrounds together for a celebration of good taste and beauty. Recalling the elegance and glamor of high French society, guests are encouraged to engage with one another in a setting with no disruptions from cars or pedestrian traffic.

We chose the catered meal option, but like all other guests, we brought along our own table and chairs, a white tablecloth and cloth napkins as well as cutlery, dishware and glassware. Even our garbage bag is white, of course.

We filled our white picnic basket with the meals Mateo had ordered weeks before. For himself, he chose the herb-crusted chicken and for his guest, (me!) the cedar-planked salmon. Each option includes an appetizer, entrée and dessert, with every bite meant to delight our taste buds. Mateo had also ordered additional appetizer and dessert samplers, to share with other guests sitting nearby or anyone strolling by or visiting our table.

The traditional napkin wave at the start of the dinner, captured by videographers recording the event for social media posts, set the convivial tone. Mateo and I toasted each other, raising our champagne glasses in unison as we settled in to enjoy the scenery, the food and all the festivities.

It didn't escape my notice that we were one of several tables garnering special interest, both from fellow attendees and the media.

Chatting with those at neighboring tables is polite and restrained. We aren't here to loudly voice political views or be disruptive. No room for snarkiness this evening! Now, if anyone had said anything offensive, I knew that I'd rise to the occasion, but nothing of that sort occurred.

I know I'm being clocked, though. I look as feminine as anyone else here in a dress, but my voice, even speaking as softly as I can, is a dead giveaway. But no matter. Mateo had said he didn't care if people identified me as being in drag. His hope was to show that a drag queen could be supremely beautiful in a subtle, feminine way. I'm serving sisterhood without being overboard about it, and that suits the occasion perfectly.

Later, as we dance in an area decorated with white streamers and balloons, I enjoyed the masculine embrace of my dinner partner. We laugh like children during the lighting of the sparklers and we spend more time than most inside the photo booth.

Perhaps the biggest surprise of the night is the number of men who seem attracted to me, winking, smiling, nodding in my direction. Supposedly straight men. But then again, one can never be too sure about how we perceive others, right? I was the living proof of that on this particular evening.

Even before we left Díner en Blanc, my phone, which I kept mostly in my white clutch throughout the evening, is buzzing wildly with notifications. Of course, both Mateo and I had taken photos and videos, but we tried to balance that with enjoying the actual event in real life, not just through the lens of a camera.

But when I take a moment to see what all the buzz is about, I have to show Mateo. There, on the event's Insta home page, the pinned post is a shot of Mateo and me, sitting close together, as I'm suggestively blowing an iridescent bubble, using one of the little toys he had brought along for some extra fun.

The caption read: "No one's going to burst the bubble of this gorgeous couple, enjoying themselves at tonight's festive Díner en Blanc. They perfectly capture the ambiance of the evening, with a special moment in time."

The same photo and caption are featured across their social media platforms, including Facebook and Twitter. But the real kick is the viral TikTok video, showing the sequence where I was blowing the bubble, which grew to an almost impossible size before suddenly bursting, ending with us giggling in pure enjoyment of the moment.

I know that being featured in such a prominent way is the first step. I have a date with Super Stardom and I will not be denied. See you at the Hollywood Walk of Fame!

LET'S TALK ABOUT SEX

B obby and I are both tired when we get to his place after our day trip to Hershey. I get cranky when I'm tired, but when a big gurl like me is trying to make a good impression, well, I know how I act. I start frontin'.

His apartment, I'll admit, is impressive. It's located within a section of the city that used to be known as the Gayborhood, but now it's been so heavily gentrified that it's hardly worthy of that name anymore. Still, it's a very nice, though very expensive, neighborhood that I can only hope to one day be able to afford.

"You're probably tired after such a long day, so how about we just relax and take it easy? No need to rush into anything," he assures me.

I'm not sure how honest he's being. I know men, and I know what they want. I also know that many men refuse to wait to get what they're after. Is Bobby different? That remains to be seen.

The truth is, I am tired, but I'm also feeling...needy. As in, sexually needy. Being treated like a lady often has that effect on me, and Bobby has done nothing other than treat me right the entire day.

"Have a seat, babe, and just take it easy. You wanna watch some TV?" He hands me the remote.

"Let me go get changed, and I'll be right back. OK?"

"Sure."

While I have some time alone, Bobby occupies my thoughts. *What are the possibilities? Can a relationship between a skinny, nerdy, white librarian and a fat, Black, dramatic Drag Queen work? And if so, what would it take?*

I continue making comparisons. Bobby's face is handsome enough, though angular, slender, even a bit jagged. My face is round, smooth, with wide eyes and full lips, often adorned with lipstick. I consider myself to be quite beautiful and men often tell me that, so I know I'm not being delusional.

Bobby's body is so thin that I wonder if he's as fragile as he looks. Can his body even handle what it would take to satisfy the woman in me? And can he handle me when I'm feeling my masculinity? That's an important question to answer, because I am not always the passive one in bed.

All these doubts. Confusion. Hesitation.

I jump when I first feel Bobby's hands on my shoulders, massaging, caressing me, but then I relax into the sensuality of the moment.

"My god, you are strikingly beautiful," he whispers. "I think you're the man of my dreams."

Sometimes, men think that men who dress in drag must automatically be transgender, or at least, totally passive. When Bobby refers to me as the "man" of his dreams, it's clear that he understands me better than most. Though there are many times when my actions scream femininity, that doesn't make me a female. I can be a feminine male, and my thoughts and actions can change depending on my feelings at any particular moment.

I've been known to play butch, and I need someone who can appreciate both sides of me.

"Tell me what you like about me." I say, challenging him, testing him.

Bobby walks around to take a seat next to me, meeting my eyes with his.

"The first time I saw you, I was struck by your outer beauty. Damn, you are a fine-looking young man."

His eyes never averted from mine, never giving me any reason to think he's being dishonest.

"I always liked men with more meat than I have on my skinny ass. I don't know. It's sexy and hot and delicious!"

His words are met with a warm smile from me.

"Then I watched you with the kids at the library and I saw your inner beauty, at least a bit of that. Kind and thoughtful, respectful of them...and encouraging them to be their true selves. That's beauty, too."

"Do go on," I tease, though his words ring true and are a breath of fresh air to me, especially after the way Twiggy has been treating me.

"And then today. You made today a beautiful, fun experience for me. I feel comfortable being with you. But more than that, I feel so turned on by you. I wanna sex you up so bad I can taste it!"

My inhibitions and doubts melt away, as Bobby takes my face in his hands, drawing me close to him, so close that I feel breathless. His kisses begin softly, but rapidly increase in intensity, like an Atlantic hurricane going from Cat 1 to Cat 5, like a train slowly pulling out of the station and then hitting 90 mph two minutes later, like a river gently rolling along its path and then suddenly turning into whitewater rapids before spilling over a majestic waterfall.

What begins as gentle nibbling on my neck turns into quick sucks on my nipples, then moving higher, breathing heavily as he plays with my earlobes and tongues my inner ear.

I'm not a passive receiver of his passion. I meet his ardor with a passionate strength of my own. Our tongues meet, twirling, caressing, slobbering, twisting, as moans escape both of our bodies. I claw at him, a tiger in heat, pulling his hair, sucking his neck, twisting his tight nipples as I cling to him.

We struggle to remove our clothes as we're tongue-tied, moving as one towards the bedroom door. Once on the bed, Bobby is on his back, legs splayed, and with a firm push, I'm inside. Ahhh, the heavenly feeling of a tight ass pulsing against my dick. It's been a minute since I felt that rush of masculinity, with Bobby writhing in pleasure, moaning in ecstasy beneath me.

Bobby doesn't climax, but he makes sure that my juicy delight has filled his house of pleasure. And then, he turns the tables, topping me as hard as I had just ridden his ass. Two versatile tops, doing what we do.

That's when I'm sure that Bobby's a keeper. *Maybe this one will last a while,* I think, drifting off to sleep.

Later the following day, when I return to Twiggy's house in South Philly, my heart sinks when I see all my belongings scattered on the front porch.

Why you gotta do me like that? I think, picking up various items of clothing and stuffing them into my bag.

I consider knocking on the door and trying to make things right, but then I decide not to bother. I hadn't made any promises to Twiggy before I moved in. I had nothing to apologize for or to explain. So, fuck him. It's going to be all right.

But now, I do need a place to stay.

Bandana Boy is a popular OnlyFans account, featuring solo sex videos, photos and chats. Subscription costs are low, attempting to keep that easy money on the flow. Guys who pay the monthly fee can access the account any time they feel like seeing me, but to watch me live, well, you gotta pay up. If your tip is enough to get my attention and say something in the comments, I might even moan your name while I'm performing.

Horny, lonely guys love when I do that for them. For just an instant, they know they're the center of my attention. And everyone else knows it, too. I know that on the other side of the screen, those dudes are blowin' their loads at the sound of hearing their name on my lips.

My name is Bandana Boy because I always wear a bandana around my neck. But lots of guys call me "Banana Boy" by mistake, and that's understandable because my banana is the largest one in the bunch.

That's another reason I'm popular on OnlyFans.

Now, I'm producing new videos, using the name "Slash." The title of the first one I'm promoting is "Slash Makes a Splash." Catchy title, right?

I just set up my phone on a tripod to shoot the videos. Keeping it simple means I have zero production costs, maximizing profits. That's how I roll.

As Slash, the bandanas are gone, a thing of the past. My costume consists of tight briefs and a pair of over-the-knee socks, making me look like I might be in a locker room, dressing to play soccer, rugby, or some other manly sport. Which, of course, is exactly what I'm about to do, though the sport I'll be playing is called sex.

I position a bowl of fruit nearby as I prepare to start the livestream. Specifically, bananas.

The screen tells me I'm now live. Hundreds of guys are already waiting, and the counter keeps going up more and more quickly. My promos worked!

"Welcome to my livestream," comes out more like a sexy growl than a greeting. I know what my fans like.

I'm sitting on a white plastic chair, legs open wide, with a pouch full of meat that's the envy of every guy watching. Those who have seen me before already know the treat they're about to receive. For others, they stand to be delighted very quickly.

"One quick announcement before I start the show. If you're any-where near Philly, the place to be this Friday night is Club Fuego. My bestie is gonna make her debut in the drag show, so bring some bucks and be sure to tip my gal Fangula. This Friday, Club Fuego. Don't forget."

"Now let's get right to it, guys. I'm kinda hungry. About to eat a banana."

I grab the smallest one and tear it from the bunch.

"Who got a really teeny peenie out there and wants to tell the whole world about your shame? And I mean a tiny dick, almost like a clit. Who got one like that?"

Again, I know my audience. Some guys get off by humiliating themselves, so I give them the space to do exactly that.

The comments start coming quickly into the chat as guys confess to their lack of size.

"Now who's gonna match that up with a big tip? Small-dicked dudes make great tippers. Prove me that I'm right!"

As the tips roll in, I'm all smiles, rubbing myself for their enjoyment.

"Come on, guys, tell you what. The first one to give me a tip over $100 gets his name written on this tiny little banana...and then I'll play with it like I'm playing with your little thing."

The chat room says:

Angelo: "My dick so tiny it gets lost in my thick hairs. Tipped you $100, Sir."

Slash: "Thanks, little Angelo, or should I call you Angie? You're kinda girly, ain'tcha Angie? I like to hear about your shrinky-dink, and so do all the manly dudes here, right, dudes?"

William: "When my little bird dick gets hard, my guy laughs and then I shrink even more. Enjoy this tip, Sir. You're worth it. I worship at your feet. Take this $150."

Slash: "William, every guy here knows that your guy is made up in your head. No one likes a dick that little, you freak."

More tips get added as I make fun of my customers. They love it!

Trent: "Say my name, please, Sir. I got $200 for you if you just whisper my name, please."

Slash: "Can't say your name till I see the cash in my tips. Till then, your name is no name, little dick dude."

I'm laughing, but then I get serious.

"If you're listening, no name little dick dude, pay up or get the fuck out. Don't waste my time with your lies."

Back to the chat:

Trent: "It ain't a lie, Sir, here's that $200 tip."

Slash: "Good boy, you're a very good boy, Trent. If you're in my area, maybe we can meet up some time, but with a dick as teeny as yours, you better bring a wad of cash for that to ever happen."

Back to my dialogue:

"Hey guys, look at this little piece of fruit, this tiny banana. Think it looks tasty?"

Slowly licking the banana from the base to the tip, I stare directly into the camera.

"This is me licking Trent's cock. See how small Trent is? Trent can't even imagine having a man-sized cock like mine."

I begin to rub the banana against my cock, straining against the fabric of my underwear. Pulling the waistband open, I push the fruit into my pouch, rubbing it against my hardness.

"Oooooh, Trent, rub your dick against a real man. You feel that, don't you, Trent?"

Then, I pull the fruit out and grab hold of an edible marker. For all to see, I write Trent's name on the skin of the banana.

"Hey Trent, are you a real man? You wanna show off how big your wallet is? You got another $200 to convince me to eat your banana dick right here in front of the crowd?"

Trent's chat shows the sweating emojis, about 5 or 6 of them, and then the magic number, another $200 from Trent, shows as a new tip.

"This is how I treat a girly man like Trent; I like to keep Trent happy, so watch this."

Licking the banana once more, I take the entire piece into my mouth, so just the tip of the base is peeking out. At the same time, I lower my briefs to show just enough to be sure the viewers know that my piece is gigantic, now swollen with desire.

I start to moan. "Who's the biggest tipper in the house?" I struggle to speak, my mouth stuffed with the fruit, that I then spit out onto the floor.

"You see, Trent, a real man like me ain't never gonna be happy with your teeny peenie."

"I need more tips to get me harder!" I whisper, then I stand and turn and lower my briefs just enough to show about half my ass. Licking my lips, I grab a larger banana from the bunch and start to tickle my asshole with it, though the audience can't see the target.

Turning to face the camera once more, I slide myself down onto the banana, a look of horny ecstasy on my face.

"Who has a bigger dick than little Trent?" I ask them. "Who wants to tip me enough for me to ride their cock?"

Now, it's time to ride the other side of the fence. Not everybody watching is submissive, of course.

The chat is jammed with messages, trying to get my attention. Tips are adding up fast. Some are small, just a few bucks, but they all add up in the end.

The chat window shows:

David Dee Dominant: "Boy, you paying attention? $500 for you if you take the biggest banana you got, write my name on it and fuck yourself in your tight ass till you shoot your cum. After 30 seconds, I disappear and take my offer with me."

That gets my attention. I can sure use $500.

"Guys, guys, guys. Keep the tips coming. But it looks like we got a real live *Dominante* in the house. Y'all see what he wants. Clap if you wanna see me obey him."

The clap emojis are showing strong.

I take the bunch of bananas and break off the two largest. On one, I write "David Dee." On the other, I write "Dominant."

The writing gets a little sloppy when I pour some lube on the fruit, then reaching behind me to prepare myself.

"Yes, Sir, David Dee Dominant. I see you. I hear you. I obey you."

My eyes widen as I pull my briefs to the side, exposing my swinging 10 inches of manhood. I spit on my cock and wipe it off, using the spit as lubricant.

Holding the fruit by the base on the chair, it's aimed upward at my pucker hole.

"Fuck me, David. Fuck me, David Dee Dominant!"

I push the first banana into me and gasp with delight.

The chat room goes cray-cray with horned-up comments:

"Fuck yourself, do it!"

"You look like a banana split! I wanna eat it!"

"All the way up inside your boy pussy!"

I ride the hard banana like I'd ride any dick. With style. I'm stroking my own meat to its greatest length, feeling the pulses of desire drawing my balls upward.

Then I lick the second banana, once more moaning David's name, then shoving that second banana into my mouth.

I can't hold back any longer. I bite the banana in my mouth in half, with the bottom piece falling to the floor. My legs tremble while I take my cock in both hands, pleasuring myself. Even gripped in both palms, several inches still extend beyond my grasp. Then, my eyes roll back as I shoot streams of cum up onto my chest, some of it splattering on the other half of the fruit, still in my mouth.

"This is for you, David Dee Dominant, and also for all you little dicked dudes that joined us tonight."

I lick the banana clean of *all that jizz*.

I end the show by sitting there, a fat banana still stuck up my ass, playing with it a little as my cock continues to leak some after-juices.

"Thanks, guys. This is Slash, your favorite boi on OnlyFans. Come back next time and don't forget to subscribe, and tell your friends about me. This show will be available for all subscribers to watch at any time. Good night, dudes!"

And then I click off the camera.

The champagne we drank at Díner en Blanc had the desired effect. By the time Mateo was escorting me into his Washington Square condo, I was horny as a motherfucker, ready to get down with my main man.

At least, that's how I thought of him. My main man. Even if it's just for tonight.

Picture the most beautiful man you've ever seen, Latino-flavor. Then, try to imagine him to be twice as beautiful. In my eyes, that's Mateo. My heart melts every time I look into those deep, liquid brown eyes. I want to disappear right into them.

Body by god. The muscular shoulders, the sculpted chest, the chiseled arms, and the tight waist. All scream masculine sensuality.

We embrace and kiss as he closes the door behind us. Instantly, we're both transformed into wild animalistic creatures, lusting for one another with passions so deep that they could not, would not be denied.

His tongue explores my lips, mouth, and ears, and my back arches as he reaches for the prize. With one quick movement, he takes the hem of my dress, lifting it over and off of me, leaving me exposed in my padded bra, panties, stockings and garter belt.

My shoes have already been kicked across the room.

"Bedroom. Now!" he orders, removing his suit jacket and pearl necklace.

Taking me by the hand, guiding me to our destination, I'm breathless, purring like a pussy.

Laying atop me, I can feel his excited manhood extending itself as the blood lust engorged him. He's pushing himself against me, trying to enter me, though he isn't even naked yet.

Turning me over, reaching for my waist, he pulls down my panties, moaning at the sight of my plump ass, massaging me, scratching me, tugging at me.

"*Puta*, you're my *puta* now, you hear?"

I lean into the pillow, again arching my back, demonstrating my desire to be taken.

I hear him unzipping his pants and tossing them on the floor, and I feel a hardness against me that shocked even a pro such as myself.

His fingers, wet with spit, push inside me, opening me, preparing me for this onslaught of hot Latino sausage. He grunts as he pushes his way inside, pausing every few seconds, feeling my ass clenching him while he probes deeper and deeper into me.

After expressing our passions, relieving all the pent-up sexual energy between us, I fall into a deep sleep, closely held by this man who's providing a sense of hope for me.

Hope for the future, hope to move beyond my current situation, hope to be somebody. An individual, yes. A Queen among Queens, yes. But also a person with a strong support system, a foundation upon which to build. This is my dream for the future.

Is it wrong to want to be owned by a man? Should I hide my true feelings just to meet the expectations of others? What's wrong with submitting to the will of a strong, masculine Latino who has needs, wants, and desires? If that's what both of us want, how is it anyone else's business to object?

I've spent years putting others first, and I have no regrets about that. Especially when it comes to my baby bro. I would die for that boy.

But now, I feel like I owe it to myself to allow myself the pleasures that feed my soul.

Mateo is everything I've dreamed about. I want him to feel that way about me. I'll do everything in my power to make that happen.

MIDGE

"Cheeses H. Christina Aguilera, gurl, you got an actual glow all about you this morning," Cobra greets me as I appear at the kitchen table for breakfast. "Somebody done gone and got herself a special man!"

There's no denying that when I'm happy, I wear my heart on my sleeve, big and bold for all to see. Today, I'd need a puffy-sleeved blouse to make enough room for all my happiness.

But there's work to be done. Tonight is my debut on stage at the club. It's been a long time realizing this dream, and I'm not one to let dreams go to waste, to disappear into thin air, like a Philly subway rat scurrying down the long, dark tunnels of the SEPTA system.

Being onstage with the renowned Midge is the cherry on top. Everyone in Philly knows, loves and respects Midge. She's earned it all.

Midge started as an attraction on the mixed martial arts circuit. Promoters viewed him as entertainment, a sideshow, a clown, not as a serious contender. Midge, however, had other ideas. He wasn't about to let years of training in judo, jujitsu and Muay Thai be ignored, only to be cast as some sort of miniature sideshow freak.

Though short in stature at 4 feet, 1 inch, this little person is fierce, in every sense of the word. During his first MMA match, held at the Rivers Casino on Delaware Avenue, the crowd wasn't exactly on his side at the start. However, his moves against his much taller, much slower, less athletic opponent soon brought out the excited rush of adrenaline from fans who would soon come to idolize him.

He could have remained a superstar on that circuit, but his plans were bigger than that. He aimed to become a star in multiple arenas, across platforms. MMA was just the beginning for him.

After that first win, he was interviewed by *The South Philly Review*, a small local publication.

The reporter asked, "You call yourself "The Midge." Isn't that somewhat derogatory?"

Midge was as quick with a comeback as he was with his moves in the ring.

"That name is a tribute to my late mother, Midge. What are you trying to imply? That it has something to do with my size?"

"I'm so sorry. I just thought..." The reporter was flustered by Midge's answer, worried that he had said something offensive.

Midge's high-pitched laughter bounced off the walls of the locker room where the interview was taking place.

"Don't worry, I'm only teasing you. My mother's name is Patricia and she's alive and well. Of course, my name is all about my size. That's what people think when they see me. I know it. They see a midget."

"Can I quote you on that?" the reporter asked.

"Sure you can. It's the truth and I'm not afraid of the truth. But let me explain. I'm glad that in polite society, people don't refer to us as midgets anymore. I'm a small person and I'm proud of that fact. But using this name is a way to remind myself and the world that oppression still exists. My community faces obstacles and I want to help the world recognize that fact, while also helping us to make progress. So if being called Midge...not The Midge, by the way...just Midge, helps, well, I'm okay with that. Next question."

That interview was picked up by the Associated Press, and Midge was already on his way to making his mark. Multiple newspapers, magazines, podcasts, and media outlets all wanted to interview the small but mighty sensation.

More matches ensued, and no opponent took Midge for granted. They recognized that he could fight. He could beat them. And that's what he did to almost every opponent.

Midge, always conscious of opportunities for self-promotion, began wearing more provocative, more revealing garb in the ring. He replaced his baggy boxing shorts with tight, revealing leggings and yoga pants.

The females were quick to notice that Midge was not only of regular size with that package between his legs, he was actually the proud owner of *El Bicho Grande*, The Big Dick.

Female fans began to flock to his matches. Men acted like they didn't notice, but who are we kidding? They noticed it. And many of them were insanely jealous of Midge. And more than a few, of course, desired him as much as the women did.

Midge didn't confine himself to building a fan base with the MMA crowd. He started experimenting with making gay porn videos, selling them on the web, directly to customers who subscribed to his Telegram account. Starting with solo videos, he progressed to performing with others. Of course, sex was the main attraction, but Midge always made sure the other sex workers in the videos never acted like it was unusual to be having sex with a person of small stature. It was important for Midge to have it perceived as totally normal and natural, which of course, it is. He refused to be objectified or fetishized.

His most popular videos were those he made with the Blonde Bulgarian Boys, two performers, calling themselves twins, who were considered "gifted," possessing "huge" talents. Viewers would often debate whether they were actually twins or not. To this day, Midge refuses to divulge that information, knowing that keeping fans guessing is the most profitable strategy.

I never saw Midge at an MMA match. I may have seen Midge perform in a sex video, or two or three. But where I got to know her personally was in a different venue, one where Midge appeared not as the mighty warrior and not as the insatiable sex actor. No, my appreciation for Midge began the first night I saw her as the hostess of Drag Queen Bingo Night at a club in Center City Philly. My friends and I had purchased a table at the event and enough bingo cards to play multiple games at once, all for a good cause. All proceeds went directly to the William Way Community Center, which first opened in the mid-70s and continues to serve as an important resource for the entire LGBTQ+ community.

Midge was dressed in vintage Dolly Parton attire that night, and she proved to be just as entertaining as the superstar she was emulating. Funny, naughty, sexy, charming. It was a delightful evening.

I won two games that night, and Midge, when seeing me for the first time as she handed me my cash prize and a bonus of a gigantic rainbow-colored lollipop that I promptly began licking lasciviously, said, "True beauty. That's what you have. I think you're going to be a star someday!"

Everyone at the table heard what she said to me, of course. Though none of us had yet done an onstage drag performance, we were all Queens in the making at that time. And while there's a tradition of Queens being catty and snarky, sometimes the comments cross the line and become hurtful. I know I shouldn't let them get to me, but I hadn't yet developed my suit of armor to protect me from the vicious ones.

"By star, she means the Death Star," Ms. Brenda, aka Bernard, said to Cammie.

"I think she mispronounced Jar Jar," Cammie replied, referring to the character from *Star Wars*.

"You know I can hear you. I'm right here," I muttered.

"Ohhh, the gurl can hear us. I'm so scurred!" Cammie said mockingly.

"Of course, she can hear us. With those ears, she can pick up signals all the way from the Space Station!"

Cammie and Brenda, laughing with delight, kept digging.

"Yes, the ears, the ears. And don't forget her teeth. They're so yellow, I heard a gold miner started digging in her mouth, searching for treasure!"

"And a caveman drew some of those prehistoric drawings inside that thing she calls a nose!"

I laugh along. It's all part of the game. Until, of course, it isn't.

Since my natural beauty far exceeds that of anyone at my table, those barbs miss the mark. To be truly effective, an insult has to contain at least a kernel of truth. There's nothing wrong with my ears or my teeth, so I could easily dismiss those comments.

At her heart, Midge is an entertainer. She loves to make people laugh, often making jokes about people in the audience. But just as often, Midge would poke fun at herself.

A few of the jokes I remember from that evening include:

Midge dragged a chair over and sat opposite a queen in the audience who was wearing open-toed shoes. "Do you know what I'm doing, doll?" she asked, as she took a jar of strawberry preserves, opened it, placed it on the floor and then stuck her right big toe into the jar.

"No, Midge, are you seasoning a strawberry daiquiri?" said the queen, not sure what the joke was, but wanting to be in on the fun.

"No, my dear, I just want everyone in the room to know that at least one person in the world has a worse case of toe jam than you do."

The audience howled!

One person called "Bingo!" but was embarrassed when she didn't really have a winner. Midge marched over and started the ringtone on her phone. Pretending to answer, having a short conversation, she then turned to the offender and said, "Honey, that was your teacher, with a reminder to do your homework tonight. She said you're so dumb, you don't even know your one times tables." Then Midge grabbed the queen's hand, patting it lightly and saying, "Don't worry, dear. We all make mistakes. Not as dumb as yours, but we do make mistakes."

Again, the audience loved it.

Later, walking around the room, sniffing the air, Midge stopped and asked a muscle queen, who was dressed in leather pants, boots, and a vest with no shirt, "Have you seen those commercials for the new products that get rid of body odor on all parts of the body?"

Mr. Leather Man said, "Yes, little one, would you like to borrow some of mine?" As he said this, he acted as if he was sniffing Midge closely.

Midge pretended to be insulted, but she had a comeback ready. "First, did you just call me 'little one?' Ohhh, can I jump in your lap, Daddy? I might be in love!"

"And by the way," she continued, "If you already have some, are you sure you read the directions? You know, you're supposed to put it ON your body!"

"But seriously, I wanted to ask if you still have the tracking number for your delivery. Because clearly, that package got lost in the mail! Phew!"

More entertainment from Midge during the Drag Bingo Night:

Upon seeing a young twink, standing about 5 feet 2 inches, Midge purred, "Guuuurlll, you are one tall drink of water. Come on over here and give lil Midge a sip!" And then Midge got down on her knees in front of the twink, opening her mouth as if waiting for a drink of "lemonade."

"I've never ever seen anyone wearing that shade of lipstick before. And I hope to god I never see it again! I mean, why did you decide you want your lips to be the same color as the mold in my shower?"

"Where in the holy fucking hell did you get those god-awful shoes? I mean...oh, hunny, didn't your mother ever teach you *anything*? Like, you walked into a store, looked around, and said 'I think I'll take those?'" Of course, the horrified look on Midge's face made it clear she disapproved of the style choice.

"May I borrow your bag for a moment? I just wanna test to be sure it clashes with everything!"

We can't take comments like those too personally. They aren't meant like that. I'm never bothered by what anyone says about my appearance, because that isn't a weak area for me.

We don't advertise our weaknesses. That makes things too easy for our enemies. The remarks that make me cringe are attacks about my family, such as my drug-addicted mother, or my absentee father, or about my lack of a formal education, or about my current state of living close to poverty. Those hurt the most. But I never, ever let anyone know. That knowledge gives them too much power over me. I will not allow that.

I cannot wait for the opportunity to work on the same stage as the Divine Miss Midge.

THE DEBUTANTE

Tonight, I'm meeting Midge in a new context: as a colleague on the club stage. Seeing that this is my debut and Midge has a lot of experience, my hope is that I can learn from her—learn more than just by watching her perform.

I feel like a VIP, walking up to the club, pulling my rolling suitcase along, with everything I'll need for tonight's performance packed neatly inside.

"Going inside in a minute. Thanks for all your help getting me ready. Love you."

I hit the button to send the text to Cobra, my true support system. Without him, the clothes wouldn't be freshly ironed, safely enclosed in plastic bags, keeping them safe in case of any unexpected spills of makeup or anything else.

There's already a line to get into the club. This'll be a big night because Midge has a huge fanbase in Kensington. Our people do show up to support their faves. In the back of my mind, I hope that one day, they'll be standing in line for me.

I walk past the line. I'm a performer tonight. Not a spectator. The bouncer ushers me inside, saying, "Oh gurl, do good tonight. Elie's expecting you to blow the house out!"

Elie. Eliud. After being with Mateo, Eliud had been pushed far back in my mind. But why can't he enjoy my show? Just because he's a player, that doesn't mean he can't be a supporter.

I guess being a newbie makes my expectations a bit unrealistic. Making my way backstage, I'm greeted by the open door to the dressing room. No one is there to provide any guidance.

I was expecting some sort of a team meeting, where the MC and the performers would go over the agenda for the night. Nope. Nothing like that. Janus isn't even there yet, as far as I can tell.

Taking a deep breath, I stand at the door, preparing to meet my fellow Drag Queens.

"Ritzy!" I shriek, a little too loudly, to the person seated at the middle table, staring intently into the lighted mirror.

"Oooh, gurl, you're lucky I just finished my eye. If you had startled me in the middle of doing one of my brows, I'd be fit to be tied."

I'm already embarrassed. Being inconsiderate isn't one of my personality traits.

"Don't worry, hon. No harm done, C'mon in. That's your chair over there."

"I'm sorry. I didn't mean to start off makin' a scene."

"If that's what you call makin' a scene, you're never gonna make it in this world. Relax, darlin'. I'm Ritzy, Ritzy Quackers. And you are..."

"Fangula. That's me, Fangula."

I stupidly repeated my name, but the truth is, I'm not really used to using it yet.

Ritzy rises from her chair, coming close for an air kiss, holding my shoulders.

"Look at you. What a beauty! My god. You could pass for a woman. You know that, right?"

"You're beautiful, too," I say, trying to make up for my clumsy entrance.

"Well, beauty isn't my strong point, but my manners are good enough to accept a compliment, so thank you. But let me ask you a question, dear," she said, going back to work applying her stage makeup.

"Fangula. I like the name, but why? If I had to guess, I'd think you would call yourself...oh, I don't know...Sleeping Beauty, or Bella, or something very feminine and beautiful."

"The name came to me one day. I kept seeing and hearing the word 'fang' and it just spoke to me. Besides, I want to go against type. I want people to see a different side of me. Fabulous. Ferocious. Fierce. Fangula conveys that idea better, dontcha think?"

Smiling, as she continues to stare at her transforming image in the mirror, Ritzy says, "I like that. I like the way you think. But don't just stand there, go ahead and unpack your stuff and start getting ready."

I have a lot to do, so I take my chair at the third mirror, the farthest from the door. Clearly, the first chair was reserved for tonight's star, Midge.

As we work on our makeup, hair, and every other detail of our look, we continue chatting.

"When Janus told me tonight's line-up, I recognized your name, but I don't know anything about you. Where're you from?"

"North Jersey, just outside New York. That's where I do most of my shows. But I'm here to visit a Philly friend this week, and I know Janus, so I asked him if he wanted me on the show tonight. I'm glad he said 'Yes' because this looks like it's gonna be a good crowd and I can use the tips."

"Speaking of tips, mind if I ask you a question? Tonight's my first night performing. I really wanna make it as a Queen. You have any advice you'd like to share? If you don't mind, that is."

"Mind? Hell no, I don't mind. First thing is, find your own voice in drag. It's about showcasing your art and using the illusion of gender, makeup and costume to create something that's meaningful TO YOU. If it stops being fun, doesn't fulfill you, or you're just doing it to be on a certain TV show, then don't do it."

"Good advice, thanks," I tell Ritzy.

"And don't believe the promises of fame and fortune. That's an illusion. Most Queens don't make much money doing drag, but we do it anyway because it lights us up inside. I'm passionate about it. I want to showcase my art publicly."

"I have high hopes, though. My friend told me I have ...what's the word?...aspirations. You think I should lower my expectations?" I ask.

"No, that isn't what I want you to do, and what I want doesn't matter anyway. This is about YOU. You can aim high, sure, but have an underlying reason for performing. Chase that dream, but enjoy the ride. If the chase is a chore, then is it really worth it? And, one more thing. Be bold. Don't be afraid to learn from others who've already gone down the path. That's why I'm glad you asked me. That tells me you value experience and learning from other queens. So, for example, do you watch the makeup tutorials on YouTube?"

"I spend hours watching them," I assure her.

"Good. Because some of the gurls come out on their debut looking like BooBoo the Fool, you know what I mean?"

"I don't want anyone calling me 'BooBoo,' that's for sure," I laugh.

A knock at the door interrupts the conversation.

"Delivery for a Miss Fangula," the young man says, mispronouncing my name as "Fan-JOO-la.

"Oh, darling, that's Fangula, as in FANG-u-la," I immediately correct him.

Handing me a perfect red rose, he exits quickly as I read the card.

"A red beauty for my Queen. Royalty sees royalty. Break a leg. I'll be watching.

Love you!

I almost start crying, knowing that I have the support of my friends, my brother, and now, a man who's very special to me. But I force myself to hold back the tears. I cannot let my emotions ruin the work I just put into applying my makeup.

There's more noise at the door as Midge rushes into the room, glances around, radiating energy and vitality. This man is a mini-tornado, constantly in motion, gesticulating with every word and smiling non-stop.

He warmly greets Ritzy as if seeing an old friend. Perhaps they are. I don't know the history between these two, if any.

"I heard you were on the list tonight, darling!" he tells me, and his sense of excitement only causes mine to grow even stronger. "I've been hoping you'd start performing since that first time I ever laid my eyes on your beauty!"

I'm taken aback that an icon such as Midge even knows that I exist. But I feel seen, validated, elevated, like maybe I actually am somebody.

Midge exudes confidence and she has a way of transferring that onto others.

"Let the transformation begin!" she exclaims, taking her seat at her station. "My favorite part of the evening is right here, right now. I love this process of changing from my masculine look and persona into my beautiful and alluring feminine side. Even if I'm the only one who thinks of me as beautiful and alluring."

Ritzy and I both laugh. Midge's antics continue as we all go about making our magic happen.

"Aahhh yes, here she comes. These lashes, this lipstick, this wig...oh my god, am I just the cutest little thing?"

There's a sudden silence.

"Girls, listen to me. If I say the words 'small' or 'little' or anything related to size, it might bother you. But please know that it does not bother me. I'm used to my size. As a matter of fact, I love my size. It's part of what makes me who I am. And in case you haven't noticed it, I am one fabulous fuckin' bitch! So enough with being coy. We're gonna have fun tonight, okay ladies?"

Like I said, Midge really is one helluva lovely person.

"Midge, do you mind when people switch pronouns when they talk about you? Is there any problem with doing that?" I ask.

"Well, I don't have my pronouns tattooed on my forehead, so I don't get offended. Especially because I live two lives; I call it 'embracing my duality.' I'm not trans; I am a man, and people call me a 'he.' But when I'm out there on stage, or anywhere in my drag motif, even I call myself a 'she.' So, love, the short answer is 'No,' I don't get offended at all. Now, it would be different if I had declared myself to be something different, and people dead-named me. Then, I'd have to fight for my rights to be called as I wish. But no worries, doll. Call me 'he,' 'she,' 'they,' 'them,' it's all good with me."

"I think a lot of us gay guys are like that," Midge continues. "We mix pronouns; we act out in exaggerated ways, and for me, that's a good thing. They used to call it 'Living Large.' And for me, that's how life oughta be."

I listen intently as I dress. In a few minutes, I'll be on stage.

"One more thing, Midge. I asked Ritzy the same thing earlier. Do you have any advice for a newbie like me?"

Midge doesn't hesitate to answer. "Steal the show. I don't mean literally, like stealing material. I mean, cause a scene. Make the eyes and ears of the audience focus on you. Give such a high-energy performance that no one can look away. On that stage, you're the star. Create a story and become a legend."

"Good advice, thanks," I say.

"There's more. Make your audience feel better than they did before they came to the show. Give them something to smile, to laugh about.

Don't be a drag, if you get what I mean. But, of course, be a drag, too. The best damn Drag Queen you can be."

Midge is making good points, as she continues, "You know one of the biggest lessons life has taught me?"

"What's that?' Both Ritzy and I want to know.

"People don't always deserve what they get, nor do they always get what they deserve."

I store that one in my memory banks. There are plenty of situations where it might be helpful to remember that bit of wisdom.

"Oh, just one piece of practical advice," Midge adds. "Learn how to sew. You'll save a ton of money. Doing drag is expensive as fuck. But don't be afraid to invest in yourself, in your dream. The more you put into it, the more you'll get out of it. I guarantee that."

Janus appears at the door. "You got two minutes, Fangula. I'm introducing you in two minutes. You ready, doll?"

I put my hand to my mouth in a fake act of worry. Then, I throw my arms wide open towards Janus.

"I can't thank you enough for giving me this opportunity. And yes, my King, I am READY!"

Standing backstage, nervously moving my weight from one foot to the other, I see an ocean of faces looking towards the stage. The audience includes artists, busboys, cashiers, dancers, entertainers, florists, grifters, husbands, investors, jokesters and jesters. In other words, people from all walks of life. All looking for, expecting...something. Maybe a moment's entertainment, maybe some future Queens looking for a mentor, a teacher. You never know who might be out there watching.

I can't see Janus from my point of view, but I hear him, admonishing the audience to show respect for the new Queen about to perform. I hear the crowd shout out, "R-E-S-P-E-C-T, RESPECT!" and then the crowd grows silent, listening to Janus.

His booming voice echoes throughout the room. "Ladies, you may know her as the Bubble Girl from Díner en Blanc, or the face of beauty seen at every gay event, every Pride parade, every Gay Bingo Night...or you might also know her as your friendly neighborhood waiter at Rico...it is my honor to introduce to you, in her drag debut, the Fabulous, the Fierce, the Fantastic FANGULA!"

I emerge from backstage, not thinking about the advice I've been given but living that advice. I know this is my moment to make the best first impression that I can and I already feel the love from the fans at the foot of the stage.

I've seen enough shows to realize that when Janus told me to prepare one song, he wouldn't be strict about it. So the DJ started playing my music, a mix of three songs, lasting almost 10 minutes.

My costume, looking like a modernized version of something that Morticia Addams might wear, shone brightly, as the black satin had embedded crystals and glitter glued galore.

Unlike Morticia, whose movements were restricted, my gown has plenty of room for me to perform kicks and struts. But the best part, in my opinion, are the multiple streaks of blood seemingly pouring down at jagged angles. When it comes to creating illusions with fabrics, Cobra, young as he is, has a genius talent.

The first 4 minutes of my performance consists of the full version of "Vampire" by Olivia Rodrigo. You know how it starts off softly and slowly, building musical tension as it leads to the crescendo ending?

I sync perfectly to the lyrics, acting dramatically, working every inch of the stage. As it gets to the song's final notes, I turn my back to the audience for just long enough to slip a couple of fake blood capsules into my mouth. Turning back to face the audience, I bite down, causing streams of fake blood to cover my lips, drip down my face, and splash down my dress, with some of the blood drops even reaching the floor.

The crowd goes WILD!

Cheers and screams of approval fill my ears as I bask in the glow of appreciation from the audience.

Throughout the song, I accept cash that the fans extend in my direction. There are plenty of ones, but in the mix are fives, tens, and even twenties. It feels good to be getting paid to perform. I even had the good sense to stash that very first tip, a crisp ten-dollar bill, into a hidden pocket of the dress. That's going to be saved and framed later.

And that was just the start of the show.

Without missing a beat, the soundtrack switches to "Padam Padam" by Kylie Minogue, which I chose to show off my dance skills. I prance about, even doing a few flips, and I use the pole on the stage to be sure every eye in the house is captivated by the sight of me.

All the while, collecting more cash, of course.

A five second pause of total silence keeps the audience in anticipation of how my show will end. I'm determined at this point to establish my name as a star.

For my rendition of "Diamonds" by Rihanna, I stand still in the center of the stage, using my face and arms to convey my emotions. Then, I slowly begin to strip, removing the straps from my shoulders, teasing the crowd with a glimpse of my bra, before carefully stepping out of the dress entirely, leaving it on the floor. My sheer black lacey babydoll negligée is very short, exposing my black stockings, garter belt and panties.

Just as the song reaches its conclusion, I turn dramatically, bending over, shaking my ass, showing the world the logo I had created, one that I hope will help me turn this performance into the start of an international brand.

Or, if it doesn't lead to international superstardom, at least it might help me earn some coin.

My logo, with red lips, blood dripping from the fangs, and the name "FANGULA" in the center is on the back of my panties. I keep that position, wagging my ass for all I'm worth, until the song fades away.

As I sweep up every dollar that's been tossed my way, some friends gather at the front of the stage, tossing my newly-designed business cards into the crowd, announcing my new website: fangula.com

There, I hope to start launching various products with my logo, including tee shirts, tank tops, coffee mugs, and whatever else I can think of.

Following the advice I've been given, I now feel like an official Queen, confident that I had stolen the show.

Out of breath with excitement, I pick up my dress from the floor, take it back to the dressing room, hanging it carefully, before telling Ritzy and Midge, "I'll be watching from up on the balcony. I can't wait to see your shows. Good luck and have fun!"

While making my way to join my friends, the Snark Sharks are making a grand entrance of their own. They're dressed to kill, and I mean that literally. Three of them had donned *JAWS*-like shark heads they were wearing on top of their already outrageously high wigs. Grey dorsal fins are attached to their backs. Seeing them, the DJ starts playing the theme from *JAWS,* as the crowd parts to make way for the approaching predators. Making the most of their entrance, the three of them circle their seats in a menacing manner, before plopping themselves down to critique tonight's performances.

Mateo has my drink ready for me. "The Snarks missed your show. Is that a good thing or not?"

"It is what it is. Ain't no tellin' what the ladies woulda thought. But I admit, I would have liked to hear their opinion of my act."

As we join Slash at Eliud's bar, Ritzy is already halfway through her first number. I don't know her work well enough to know if she's just having an off-night, but her decision to sing "Memory" (the Elaine Paige version from *Cats the Musical*) and Taylor Swift's "Beautiful Ghosts" from the movie version of *Cats*, was falling a flat with the audience.

The songs are beautiful, but somehow, the vibe just isn't there. And why did Ritzy decide to wear what looked like an opera singer's gown rather than something that would have been more "purrfect?" I wonder.

The Snark Sharks have their way with Ritzy, tearing her apart bit by bit, like any wounded prey. You know what they say. We eat our own. Even though Ritzy sometimes joins the Sharks, they show no mercy.

Ru-Barb: "Don't understand why Ritzy left that trail of cracker crumbs on the floor. Ain't nobody callin' her back for an encore. Not after that mess of a show."

Nepharious: "Imma be honest. She ain't no Catwoman. But I do hear she puts on one helluva show in the back alley, with the rest of the ferals. The boy cats are gonna be out there any minute now, and we'll be hearing the screeching all the way up in here."

Miss Dee Eyed: "Where's the litter box? Where's the catnip? Where's the exit? I gotta find my way the hell outta here!"

Ru-Barb: "I got a question. Who let that cat outta the bag? And even more importantly, who's gonna let the dawgs out and chase that mangy thing straight outta here?"

The gurls scream with laughter.

LIFE AND DEATH

When Janus introduces Midge, everyone's ready for the party to get re-started. Not one to disappoint a crowd, Midge is a mini-Miley, coming in like a "Wrecking Ball," swinging across the stage, singing the iconic lyrics immortalized by Ms. Cyrus. She embodies the youthful vitality and sexual energy that was Miley's persona at the time that video was created.

The air fills, dollar bills floating everywhere, like confetti, as the crowd favorite entertains the hundreds present for the show. Midge, looking divine in her costume of a floral bra with a matching skirt resembling a very, very short sarong, then channels Bette Midler, aka The Divine Miss M, in her Broadway hit, *Clams on the Half Shell Revue*. Indeed, she does a short medley of Midler hits, including "Boogie Woogie Bugle Boy," "Do You Want to Dance," "The Rose," and "Wind Beneath My Wings."

This is entertainment at its best. I'm captivated by Midge's artistry in creating an image of "Drag Extraordinaire," as is the entire audience crowding the club.

Bringing the energy level back up for her finale, Midge ducks behind the curtain, where Janus is waiting to help her with a costume change. It takes a minute, but it's worth the time to recreate Cher's iconic look for Midge's next performance, lip-syncing "If I Could Turn Back Time."

I'm cheering, delighted at the sight of Midge wearing a gigantic Cher wig that almost touches the floor, and the tight, sheer bodysuit under her leather jacket.

Strutting the stage as if she's entertaining the sailors on the deck of an aircraft carrier, Midge is Cher. The audience joins her in dancing and singing to this crowd favorite. Midge brings the act to a bang-up conclusion with her rendition of Cher's monster hit from the late 90s, "Believe."

The performance is magical, mythical, and most of all, profoundly entertaining. Midge is indeed a Queen among Queens, a delight to the senses. I couldn't applaud loudly enough.

Once the show ends, Janus asks for everyone's attention.

"Ladies, I know you want to get back to your dancing, your drugging, your drinking and your whatevering," he begins, as the crowd laughs along. "But I have one very important announcement. In two weeks, Club Fuego will host our very first Drag Wars competition. It's my pleasure to tell you that the grand prize winner will receive recognition as the first Drag Wars winner, a cash prize of $1000, and will take home the cherished Pink Tiara."

This announcement has my full attention.

"Our judges will be the one and only Harloweena; where are you, my dear? Wave at me."

The crowd applauds for our hometown icon, Harloweena.

"The second judge will be the very selective Queen of the Car Lot, who goes by the name...come on, you all know her...Miss Carlotta Sales. I'm sorry that Carlotta isn't in attendance tonight, but she is guaranteed to show up for the judging...if she wants to get paid, that is."

Again, the audience can appreciate the desire for a paycheck, so they applaud at that line.

"And the third judge will be that entertainment juggernaut, the mini-maestro of the stage, our very own Midge. Come on out for a bow, Midge!"

The hooting and hollering for Midge was never louder.

"And, one final announcement. We already have our line-up of queens for the competition. In two weeks, the first semi-final will feature Divinity Thee Goddess vs The Lady Claw!Dia vs a newcomer that you just saw this evening, the Fabulous Fangula!"

My screams of delight got the attention of everyone near me. My first performance, my debut, and I've already been selected to appear in a competition. From the stage, Janus points in my direction, winking and smiling. This was one of the best nights of my life, ever!

Janus finishes with, "Next week, we'll announce our second trio of semi-finalists. Till then, my sweeties. See you all next week!"

With a flourish, Janus disappears from the stage and the Friday night party continues

At the bar, my personal celebration is going strong. This is a night to drink till I drop. I'm surrounded with love and affection from my friends and with respect for my abilities as a performer. A moment to enjoy.

"Whaddya think about competing against Divinity?" Mateo asks, just before I check my phone, expecting to see the latest posts on my Instagram and other social media accounts, since friends were sending plenty of photos to my brother, who has access to all my accounts.

But no, that wasn't what I saw on my iPhone. Instead, three frantic text messages from Cobie were demanding my immediate attention.

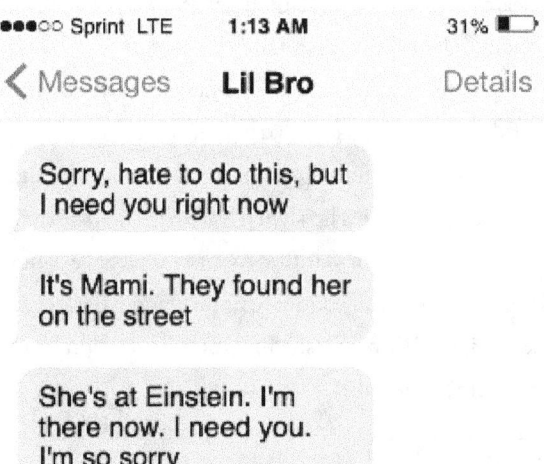

"Mateo, look at this," I say, holding my phone in front of him. "Go grab my dress. Please! I gotta go right now. If Cobie is this upset, then I know it's bad."

Einstein Hospital, just off Broad Street on Old York Road, is a short drive away. Mateo parks while I rush inside, probably looking like I need immediate medical attention, with "blood" splattered all over my dress.

I try to explain to the person at the Admissions Desk, but my words are slurred, jumbled, and probably nonsensical.

Luckily, Mateo comes in quickly and helps to explain the situation.

"We're looking for...what's your Mami's name?"

"Crissy...Cristina Maria Hernandez Pacheco."

"No one admitted by that name," the lady tells us, after doing a quick search through the hospital's files. "Maybe she's still in the waiting room. Right down that hall."

Not waiting for anyone, not even Mateo, I rush down the sterile hallway of the hospital, pushing past a set of doors and see Cobie...little Carlito...seated on a folding chair, not far from a hospital gurney.

A muffled cry escapes his lips when he sees me, and he quickly looks away, averting his eyes, not wanting to make direct eye contact.

Walking towards him, I suddenly understand what I'm seeing.

"Is she all right? Why isn't she in a room? How long has she been waitin' out here in the hall?"

I'm not really expecting an answer, certainly not from Lito. How would he know any of that?

He stands up from the chair, slumping, telling the ground, "She already been gone. She never had a chance in here. They just let her be right there, all alone, and ain't nobody by her side till I got here."

Eyes filled with tears, he looks at me for the first time.

"You understand? She be gone. Goddamn it, she already been gone."

"Gone? Whaddya mean, gone?"

And that's when the truth stands tall in front of me and smacks me right in the face.

"MAMI!! No, you can't be gone! You was about to get yourself all straight. Remember, you told me, right there at the El, you swore to god in heaven you was done with all this shit!"

I hear Mateo approaching me before I feel his arm on me.

"They let her out here to die!" I scream at him. "She died here all alone, all alone, oh my god, she died all alone."

"Shhhh, babe. Shhhh. I know. I know." Words meant for comfort did not hit their mark.

Instead, I pull myself away from his embrace, stumbling towards the gurney.

I feel dizzy, confused, angry, hurt, as I look at my Mami's lifeless body, her face still uncovered.

Instead of continuing my tantrum, I hold my rage in check, remembering that this scene will live forever in the minds of both Carlito and me.

Brushing away my tears, I stare at her, horrified at what she had become. I turn and gesture towards Cobra, my little Cobie, asking him to join me in front of our mother.

His body trembles against mine, as we stand there, our little family, looking at our mother, who had betrayed us so many times, and yet, she was the one who had brought us into this world.

I take Cobra's hand in mine, squeezing it firmly, trying to show the strength that I think he needs from me.

"My god, Mami, look at what you did to yourself. So different now. Nothing like the young, beautiful woman I remember from not all that long ago."

Cobra's hand squeezes mine back.

Staring at her, lifeless, I know that her life had actually ended long before this night.

"*Hermano*, I want you to listen to me real good. One day soon, someone in some office is gonna write some words on a piece of paper. That'll be her death certificate. But whatever that person decides to write, I don't want you to pay it no mind. Because I'll tell you right now what killed Mami. They might say it was drugs, or she had a heart attack, or something else, but here's the real fact of the matter. Mami was killed by a society that just didn't give a fuck about people like her. She never had a chance. The pain of her life cut so deep, that she didn't see no future for herself. And that's how she ended up here, like this."

Cobra nods, sobbing, maybe understanding for the first time that this is our reality, but it doesn't have to be like this. Life can be different. It should be different. And I make a promise to myself right then and there that I'll do everything in my power to make life different for us.

Me and my brother. We're gonna rise above this. I swear to mother fuckin' god, we are gonna rise!

MAY THE PRIDE BE WITH YOU

S tuck outside of Twiggy's house with nowhere to go, I debate with myself for a moment. Since I took a huge chance by moving to Philly with only an offer from a stranger on Grindr for a place to stay, I wasn't sure I wanted to take such a big chance again.

One idea is to text Bobby, which would probably result in an offer to stay at his place. I think it's too soon for that. We might ruin a good thing if we get too serious, too soon.

Another idea is to contact Ruby. She's been almost like a mother to me. Should I ask her for even more help? When does a person feel that the puppy that's tagging along has become too great of a burden? I don't want to be a lost puppy in Ruby's life. I have more self-respect than that.

Twenty minutes later, I hop out of my Uber, standing at the entrance to Fabrizio's Fabrics. Before walking inside, I put on my mask of self-confidence, hoping to hide the quivering fear of failure that, when discovered, provides an easy target for scammers and the like. I think I can trust the man in here, but I've learned to be only cautiously optimistic, at best.

A customer leaves just as I enter, leaving the store's owner and me to have a private conversation.

"Jalen!" he greets me, as if seeing an old friend. I'm surprised and delighted at his warm welcome.

"Hello, Janus! I hope you're not busy. I'm not here as a customer right now. I was hoping we might be able to talk. You know, man to man. Or, something like that."

Janus ignores my attempt at humor, possibly because my face betrays the serious nature of my visit.

"Hmmm, why don't we make sure we can talk uninterrupted, then. I could use a coffee. You?"

"Sounds good to me."

Janus turns the "OPEN" sign on the front door to show that the store is "CLOSED." We walk half a block north and enter the diner on the corner, taking a booth as far from the door as possible.

Some people inspire confidence, giving others the space to express themselves openly and freely. I think Janus might be one of those people, but I proceed cautiously at first. I've been wrong about people before.

My hope is that I can tell Janus anything, that I'm in a safe space and that no matter what, he'll be non-judgmental and supportive.

I start at the very beginning, with the train trip from Baltimore, watching his reactions. Once I begin telling the story of the past few days, since I left Baltimore, I can't stop. Janus sits across from me, eyes focused solely on me, listening with an intensity that few could match.

The train ride with Ruby, moving in with Twiggy, Drag Story Hour at the library, the day at Hershey with Bobby, and the night after. There was no reason to hide anything. I needed to make real connections in my new town, and honestly, it felt good to confide fully in someone.

Once I finished, I wait for his reaction.

And wait.

"Meg, I'll take a refill here," he says, telling the waitress he's ready for more coffee.

Somehow, when he turns his attention back to me, I feel engulfed, like I'm the only other being in his world. That's the intensity of his attention. I've never experienced this sensation with any other person.

"Jalen, when I look at you, and when I hear what you've been through, I don't see a person struggling. I see someone in the process of overcoming obstacles. And you know what else I see?"

He didn't wait for me to answer.

"I see an entertainer. A born entertainer. A star in the making. The potential you have to reach others with your abilities is unlimited."

The quizzical look on my face gives away my confusion.

"I know you expected a different kind of answer, but we can deal with your problems fairly easily, I believe. That's why I'd rather concentrate on something more important."

"What's more important than what I just told you? I'm basically homeless, so that's my biggest worry right now."

"Humor me. I already have a possible solution for that. Let that go; put it out of your mind and do something for me, right now."

"Do...what?"

Leaning in close, grabbing hold of my side of the table, Janus whispers. "Show me the entertainer in you. The person you're hiding from me, but I'll be honest, Ruby told me all about you. And if Ruby believes you have special qualities, then so do I."

After taking a breath, Janus continues, "Show me your heart, your soul. Don't hold anything back. If I'm even halfway right, you can win, well, I'm guessing there's about 2-dozen folks in here. Let's turn those 2-dozen people into fans. Win them over with your talent."

I have no reason to hesitate. I know I'm good. Better than good. My voice was known to grace the presence of the church-going folks in Baltimore, first as a member of the choir and later as soloist.

Getting up, I walk to the front of the diner. This gurl is not going to start a solo in the "back of the bus."

One of my favorite songs, and one that shows my vocal talents, is "Lift Every Voice and Sing." There's a good reason why it's been called the "Black National Anthem," with stirring notes and words of inspiration. Written as a hymn by James Weldon Johnson and set to music by his brother, J. Rosamond Johnson, this song brings out my raw emotions.

As Janus had expected, all activities in the diner came to a standstill during my performance. No chattering conversations, no clattering of dishes, no calling out orders to the kitchen, nothing. All eyes and ears are attuned to me. My voice, my presentation, everything is stellar. Can a star be born in a diner? I think the answer is Yes.

A standing ovation from almost everyone in the diner, providing a thrill that every performer will recognize. Janus is on his feet, applauding, smiling, and appreciating my talents. Oh, what a feeling!

The waitress approaches, pulling the check for our table from her pocket, waving it at me and saying, "Order up, honey. Anything you want. It's on the house today. My treat!"

Not one to turn down a free meal, I order the biggest stack of blueberry pancakes they could make. With a side of bacon. Satisfaction!

"I have two propositions for you, Jalen," Janus tells me. "First, I want to invite you to be in our drag show this Friday night. You know Club Fuego?"

"I'll find it," I assure him.

"Second, I want you to meet someone back at the store. I texted her and told her about your housing issue. It just so happens that her housemate moved to Canada about a month ago, and she's looking for s new roomie."

"Ok, one question. Are we talking about a 'her/her' or a 'him/her'? You know what I mean."

Janus laughed. "You decide when you meet her. I don't label people like that. Her name's Divinity. Divinity Thee Goddess."

Just from her name, I like her already.

Even out of drag, there's no question that I'm flamboyantly femme. I'm not trying to be anything other than my true self. When I see

Divinity standing at the door of the shop, I feel a kindred spirit. This gurl is looking fine!

The first detail I always check— the nails. Hers are impeccable, beautifully painted with intricate designs on each. She raises her hands to her face when she sees us, just as I would, expressing pleasure but at the same time showcasing the work of her manicurist.

Hers is a look that's designed to look casual, while still elegant enough for a photo shoot at any moment.

Introductions are made, air is kissed, hands are fluttered. A casual meeting of two very fabulous queens.

Only a few details are needed to start, in order to decide whether we'd be compatible in the same house.

"You seeing anyone on the regular, or are you a tramp like me?" Divinity wanted to know. "I just wanna know if I should expect different random men running naked through the house every morning."

Laughter ensues.

"I enjoy long walks on the beach, reading Renaissance poetry, and drinking my herbal tea quietly by the fireplace every evening," I answer.

All three of us are now laughing comfortably. A match has been made.

We set out for my new home, living with Divinity Thee Goddess, in a two-bedroom, two-bath apartment in a section of Philly called University City.

"Lots and lots of college boys around here. You'll see," Divinity informs me, adding, "You know. In case you're ever in need of something quick and casual."

"Oh, this gurl got some needs, for sure," I answer, knowing that the two of us will get along fabulously.

"I heard you're going to be in the show at the club on Friday. Who will you be singing?" she asks.

I have some decisions to make. I want to make an impression that people won't easily forget.

Beyoncé springs to the front of my mind. Renaissance.

Divinity and I discover a common interest, when she starts telling me about her Drag Queen Story Hour appearances.

"Oh, you must come this week!" she tells me, after I describe my experience at the branch library.

"I've got one scheduled for the Main Branch on Wednesday. It's a big event. You'll love it; I'm sure. And I can always use more queens to help out."

The Main Branch of the Free Library of Philadelphia is an imposing building on the Benjamin Franklin Parkway in Center City Philly. The cavernous main floor provides plenty of spaces for different queens to be reading and entertaining different groups at the same time.

On the day of the event, two other queens, Wilma Tsetse Fly and Miss Pushy Galore, are getting into costume at our place. *Our place.* I like the sound of that. It didn't take long for Divinity to make me feel welcome. It does feel like my place, too.

As we transform ourselves from glamorous men into even more glamorous queens, Divinity is telling us about our reading groups, and handing us our books. In the days prior, we all had the opportunity to practice, by accessing the books we'll be reading online..

We form a Pride mini-parade when we leave the apartment, walking down to the waiting Range Rover, in which Eliud will drive us to our destination. *This man has patience*, I'm thinking, as four Chatty Cathys speak non-stop throughout the drive. Somehow, he keeps track of every conversation, joining in with good humor, while providing us with a safe ride to the Library.

"You're coming in, aren't you, honey?" Divinity asks Elie.

"You know I am, babe. I got my coloring fingers all ready!"

"Coloring fingers? What?" I ask, sounding more rude than I had intended.

"Pridezilla, this ain't no ordinary Drag Queen Story Hour. This is the main event! You'll see as soon as we walk in and start setting up. Today's theme is 'Over the Reading Rainbow with Bluebirds Flying' and we're gonna help these children, and some adults, use their imaginations and reach high up beyond the rainbows."

The event showcases Divinity's Type-A personality traits to the core. She demands perfection, first from herself, and then from those surrounding her. Today, she has the highest expectations for all us queens to deliver the goods, to read well, to entertain and to provide a warm, friendly environment for those in attendance.

"But what does coloring have to do with Story Hour?" I whisper to Wilma.

"Divinity has turned this into a full-on family drag experience. Some of us will be reading stories written for the young folks to the kids. That's like the traditional Drag Queen Story Hour, but Divinity has taken it well beyond that. You're gonna see older kids here, too. So, of course, you don't want them to get bored with little kiddie stories. For them, we have manga and anime books. Divinity always checks in advance, along with the professional librarians, to be sure everything is age-appropriate. Of course, LGBTQ+ content is allowed, but nothing too sexual or violent."

"Wow!" was all I could think to say, at the moment.

"Wait, there's more. When Divinity saw that the adults who brought their kids were left with nothing for them specifically, she had a brilliant idea. She added Grown-Up Story Time, providing coloring sheets and pencils, and the adults just raved about it. You know they do make coloring books for adults, and some of them have very intricate designs. Parents love them!"

Tented areas with banners and tables filled with books are scattered throughout the main floor of the library.

"Ok, ladies. Find your matching color. That'll be your station. Books and other supplies might still have to be unboxed and we start in 20 minutes sharp. So get out there and be a Queen!" came the instructions from Divinity.

Prior to meeting at our apartment, everyone had been instructed to wear costumes that included a particular bright color, and of course, wigs and makeup were designed to complement the main hue.

Divinity is in pink. She, looking divine. She seems to float about the library, headed to her pink station, where she'd preside over the group of grown-ups, listening to a chapter from a popular book as they melt their cares away, concentrating on coloring instead of the worries of the outside world. Today, she's reading from *Pageboy: A Memoir* by Elliott Page.

Wilma, dressed in red, rushes to the red station, ready with the three books she'll read to the youngest children, average age of 5. She loves picture books and can add details to the stories as she directs the attention of the kids to the gorgeous illustrations.

Pushy Galore, all aglow in her bright green outfit, has books for children in the primary grades, with text, pictures and plots that this age group will find engaging.

I make a beeline for the purple station. My lavender wig and bright purple eye shadow, with dark-purple lipstick and jewelry to match my manicured nails, all complement my royal violet gown with matching heels. For the middle grades group that'll gather with me, Divinity has provided manga and anime coloring pages, sure to capture the interest of the kids and keep them involved in an activity.

Three books are in my hand, and I wonder which to read first. *Wandering Son*, by Takako Shimura is possibly the most famous manga about trans people, with a beautiful story to tell. *The Bride Was a Boy by Chii* is light and funny, contrasting with other stories that tend to be gritty and tense.

Boys Run the Riot by Keito Gaku, the first in a series of 4 books, tells the story of two boys who bond over male fashions, leading them to develop their own fashion brand. Loving fashion myself, I decide this is the best story to begin with.

Of course, these are full-length books, so my presentation will be limited to the beginning of the book, allowing time for these kids to read later on their own and color some of the illustrations.

My intent is to introduce them to stories that give a positive perspective on LGBTQ+ storylines and characters, as well as to entertain them with my style and wit.

Looking around, I see that Divinity has drawn a rather large crowd, and even from here, I can tell that she's enjoying herself immensely. Strutting through the crowd, as some are already immersed in coloring, she's reading from Elliott Page's autobiography, dramatically gesturing as she reads selected passages.

Everyone attending the event has a reason to be there. I can't know what everyone is thinking, but I do notice that it's very easy to make personal connections. It's almost as if they're starved for some attention, as well as enjoying the brief respite from whatever personal problems and responsibilities they might have. The same is true for both the youngsters and the adults, though it's more pronounced in the adults. Of course, I know how distantly we treat strangers in public. Most of our lives, we're ignored by most of the people around us, whether we're on a bus, walking along the street, in a park, or anywhere else. There's a reason for this, but as a society and as individuals, we pay a price for our supposed privacy.

Just before I begin to read, a mother approaches me, holding her son's hand.

"Lady, I'm sorry, I don't know your name. This is my son, Jake. I'm Jennifer."

"So very nice to meet you, Jennifer. I'm Pridezilla. And who is this handsome fellow you have here?" I'm smiling at Jake, who doesn't return the gesture. He's looking at the floor, making a motion with his right fist, clenched tightly closed.

"Oh Pridezilla, what a lovely name you have!" she tells me. "Jake is on the spectrum and non-verbal. He pulled me over here because he's drawn to the color purple and of course, you caught his attention. Would you mind if he sits with your group? I'll stay close by to be sure he behaves, but I don't think he'll give you any trouble."

"Of course, he can join us. Find a seat, Jake."

His mother walks him to an empty chair, but Jake chooses to sit cross-legged on the carpeted floor instead.

It's fun to read the story of Ryo and Jin to the group around me, as I watch their young faces reflect their emotions, listening to the story of the two boys and their adventures.

Questions, of course, are always welcomed.

Xavier asks, "Miss Pridegilla, are you gay?"

Trying not to chuckle, I answer, "Well, Xavier, first, my name is Pridezilla. Like Godzilla, you know him, right?"

Xavier laughs and covers his eyes, but he knows I'm not upset.

"And yes, I am gay. I'm proud of who I am. I want everybody to be proud of who they are. You understand that?"

"Yes, Miss Pridezzzzzzzzzilla!" he replies, emphasizing the correct way to say my name.

Carole Ann joins in the conversation. "My two moms are gay and I love both of them!"

"Oh sweetie, that's beautiful," I tell her.

"I thought your name was Bridezilla, like the ladies that my dad likes to watch on TV," adds Cooper. "But now I get it. Your name is about pride, being proud of who you are."

"Exactly!" I beam at the entire group.

Kids this young, already accepting and understanding, could provide examples for many adults I know.

Once I finish reading, the kids select coloring pages and set to work on their projects. I see Jake still seated, fidgeting a bit, by himself on the floor. I grab two coloring sheets from the table, getting down on the floor to meet Jake at his level and start using a big purple marker to color one of the sheets. I don't bother to color within the lines. If there's one life lesson I've learned, it's that it's perfectly okay to draw and color outside of the lines.

A faint smile shows on Jake's face as he grabs a marker, also purple, and scribbles on the sheet.

I don't know if I made Jake feel joy today, but he has undoubtedly given me great joy, just by his very presence with us today.

Suddenly, a loud commotion is coming from the entrance to the library. Loud voices. Thumping footsteps. My heart jumps.

Three white men, dressed in combat fatigues, carrying flags that show their Nazi affiliation, are marching in, chanting "Death to Drag Queens! Death to Drag Queens!"

I'm horrified, scrambling to my feet. My first thought is to protect the kids, so I call for them to get behind me. I'm prepared to fight.

But they don't come in my direction. Instead, they head for Trinity's area, chanting and waving their flags. Something triggers one of them, who charges at Divinity with the point of the flag pole aimed in her direction. Scenes from the January 6 insurrection at the US Capitol flash through my mind.

Eliud springs from his seat, running directly at the man about to attack Divinity. Pushing the flag pole to the side, he avoids being impaled and tackles the man to the ground, pinning him firmly, making sure he cannot move. Security from the library arrives, taking over the situation and removing the three intruders.

As they're leaving our area, I hear one of the Nazis hollering, "Where are the unicorns? I came here to kill a unicorn..." and then his voice disappears into nothingness.

I'm shaken, as are many others. Divinity, however, seizes the moment, calling all four groups together.

"Please listen to me, everyone. First, I want to be sure that everyone's okay. Did anybody get hurt? If so, let us know right now, please."

No one was physically injured. I'm standing with everyone else, just now realizing that Jake has been holding my hand throughout the episode.

"This was an assault. An assault on our rights to be here. And this is why we do what we do. We cannot, and we will not, allow people like that to push us around, to take away our rights and to scare and intimidate us."

The group begins to applaud.

"I'm pressing charges against them. I hope the Free Library will join me in pressing charges. But even if I have to do it myself, I'm not letting it go."

"I'm pressing charges, too!" I shout in support.

"And Eliud, oh my god, Elie, come up here with me. Everybody, this is Eliud and he's my hero. Not just today, but today he did something so special. I'll never forget this and thank you so much."

Everyone applauds Eliud, who seems surprised by the attention.

"So listen, everyone. We were already nearly at the end of our scheduled time, so let's call it a day for now. But I hope to see all of you back here for the Next Drag Queen Story Hour. We love all of you! And thanks to my sisters, Pridezilla, Pushy Galore and Wilma Tsetse Fly for being with us today. Thank you, everybody!"

As we gather our things before leaving, I see that my hands are still shaking.

HAVE YOUR CAKE AND EAT IT

Doors open. Doors close. Sometimes, they swing open gently, inviting a person to experience something new, exciting, life-altering. And if that person accepts the invitation, they may find that they made a good decision. Or not. And if not, they may back away.

Other times, doors swing shut with a thud, leaving no escape. A final decision has been made, either by us or for us. The sounds of those doors ring the loudest in my ears, for there is no way to move into reverse.

A door opens. A text message is received, inviting me to an event. A drag art event. I can accept the invitation or choose to decline.

A door closes. When I go to the kitchen for breakfast the day after Mami dies, Cobra isn't there. No greeting of "Cheery Hoes," or something similar. I'm left alone and in silence. Though the breakfast table has been set, this routine has been brought to its conclusion. Perhaps permanently. Perhaps not. This is a door that closed gently, perhaps to swing open once more.

A door slams. Mami died last night. No returning to those nights when I was both embarrassed and relieved to see her, performing her zombie dance on Frankford Avenue. Ashamed to see her in that deluded, drug-fueled state. Yet relieved to know she was still breathing, and not lying in a park somewhere, possibly drawing her last breath.

I hated her. I hated what she had become. I hated her for abandoning me and Carlito, and for the fact that she never even got to meet him in his life as Cobra. I hated that she wasn't at my first show. And now she won't be there when I have my final show.

I hate her because she couldn't see beyond her own bleak future, to have hope for what her children might become. I hate her because she gave up on us. I hate her because she gave up on herself.

But still, I love her. I love her because I wanted to make her proud of me. I love her because she taught me how to make it in this neighborhood. I love her for giving me an example of what not to become.

I hate her.

I love her.

I wish I had more time to really know her.

Standing in the empty kitchen, hearing the water from the faucet drip, drip, drip, the sound of poverty. I can't fix it myself. There's no extra money for a plumber. The landlord never shows up except to collect the rent.

Drip, drip, drip.

I feel my life dripping away. Each drop eventually reaches the drain, going...where?

I'm a drop. Floating somewhere, being swept up by something greater, something more powerful than myself. It's impossible to go against the flow. I don't even know if this is a good thing or a bad thing. I don't even know the direction in which I'm being taken. But the forces are too great.

How do I reflect these feelings into my artistry?

Fangula. The blood. Liquid blood, also in droplets. Flowing down, always down. Why? Is it inevitable that we all gather into a pool of liquidity, types seeking similar types? What happens when B+ meets A-? When the blood types don't match? Does the blood still mix? Coagulate? Or is it more like a war?

The bare lightbulb in the plain receptacle in the kitchen goes out with a pop. I close my eyes, wishing to be transported to some magical sphere. But this isn't a movie. It isn't a fantasy. There is no magical escape for me.

The shadows now cast about the kitchen appear ominous. Why do I have such a bad feeling about the future? Is it based on anything real? I decide to seek my refuge. Over to Slash's house I go.

Through the alleys, always stopping for the Sign of the Cross at Jamal's kicks, forever dangling and twisting, the laces looking worn and filthy.

Looking up, I can almost hear Jamal's laughter over at my house, as we talk about cartoons, our favorite new videos, our pro-wrestling heroes.

"Your Mami makes the best *quesitos y bizcochos*," I hear him telling me. I smile at the thought. How many times did Mami make treats for us? I know Jamal would rather stay over at my house than at his own.

But of course, Jamal only exists in my memories now—unlike my feathered friend, who is all too real. He seems to recognize me now as a food source, fluttering to the ground, searching for sunflower seeds. I do not disappoint him. He makes several flights back up to the nest, and I can hear the crying of his newborn babies.

"Congratulations, Rojo. You're a Papi now." How about that! I wish Jamal had lived long enough to experience whatever kind of family he would have wanted.

In my mind, I hear a direct message from Jamal. Don't ask me how. I can't explain it. But I can hear his voice, right now, telling me "I have to go back now, back to my safe place. Don't worry about me, Donnie. I'm good now."

Slash opens the door to his apartment, with an extra-long towel wrapped around his waist. That usually means he's in the midst of filming, or had just finished.

"It's okay for me to come in? I don't wanna disturb you or nothin'."

"You ain't disturbin' me none, you already know," he admonishes me, pulling me into a big bear hug.

"I'm so sorry to hear about your Mami. She was always good to me."

"I know she was, thanks."

"I remember so many times bein' up at your house. God, we had some fun up in there."

"Yeah, like remember that time we went to the park to chill and that orange tabby cat followed us back to my house?"

"And we asked your Mom, 'Can we keep it?' and she said, 'Hell, naw, we ain't keepin' no damn alley cat up in here. It's bad enough I got you two pussies hangin' around the house all day!'"

That's a good, happy memory.

"And then your brother walks in, sees the cat, and says, 'What the hell! You gotta be kitten me!'"

"He was quick with the puns, even back then!" I agree.

"And then, damn if he didn't keep that damn cat and he named it Kitten, and your Mami ended up loving that little guy."

It feels good to giggle at some warm memories, especially so close after losing Mami.

"I always liked coming to your house to eat. My Mom, well, her cookin' wasn't nothin' special at all. But your Mami, well, she made the best *quesitos y bizcochos*."

Hearing Slash say the exact words I had just heard from the spirit of Jamal sends a chill through me.

Changing the subject, I tell Slash, "Cobra ain't even stay for breakfast this morning. And you know, that's a tradition with us. I'm kinda worried."

"Give the boy some slack, Donnie. He got a lot on his plate right now. And on top of all the stress he's under, now he just lost his Mom. I wouldn't be too worried about missing one breakfast."

"Maybe you're right. I just think it's a bad sign. But I have to give him some time to deal with things in his own way."

"Now, let me tell you why I'm really here. You know I count on you for all the tech stuff. Guys loved the logos you designed, but I wanna take this beyond just a business card. The website is up and running. How cool is it that I actually got the right name for my site? Anyway, I need help creating some merch with the logos on there. You got some time right now?"

"Let me clean up first. Need a quick shower. Just finished up a session on my OF."

That's when I notice the streaks of strawberry juice running down the length of his scar, and I realize how he must have been teasing his audience with more fruit.

And then I see the cake and say, "Holy Mother of Cheeses, as Cobra might say, you sat in that cake and splooged it, right? And don't lie, you know I'll watch it for myself later!"

"Gurl, I sat myself down on that cake and smooshed it first—cake on my cakes. And the guys watching? They ate it up. If they had been here in the room with me, I know a bunch of 'em woulda ate that cake right outta my ass!"

He continues telling me about his porn session, saying, "One dude kept textin' at me, 'Let them eat cake! Let them eat cake!' I texted back, asking 'who's them?' but the dude didn't seem to know who he was talkin' about. I think he's some weirdo, but he did tip me good, so who cares, right?"

"So now, you know why I really, really need a shower right now," he tells me, laughing as he drops the towel and heads for the shower.

Damn, that cake on cake sure does look tasty!

PRIDEZILLA PERFORMS

I'm not worried about doing my first show at Fuego. I have plenty of experience on the stage. I know that I look good and I sound damn good. It's time someone showed these Philly queens what Baltimore can bring to the stage.

This dressing room is tight, but I've had to squeeze myself into smaller spaces, that's for sure.

I'm the only one here. Janus told me that it was just going to be me and a queen named Lady Starr Kissed, but Starr called out at the last minute. Instead of replacing her, Janus is counting on me to carry the night. I can do it. Self-confidence is one of my strong suits.

My performances aren't meant to be imitations. Yes, I cover big hits from big stars, and yes, I have seen them perform their hits, both in concert and on video.

While I adore their performances, those belong to the original star. I don't want to be the perfect imitation. Bringing my own flavor to the performance is what makes my shows unique.

I do lip-sync if a certain song I want to perform doesn't suit my vocal talents. I see no harm in that at all. But I won't copy anyone's exact choreography, or wear their exact same costume. Not my style. I see plenty of the gurls doing just that. Which is their right. It just doesn't work for me or go with what I'm trying to do.

Since I'm doing double-duty tonight, and this crowd doesn't know me, I make a last-minute decision to add two numbers by one of my all-time favorites.

Miss Diana Ross.

At times like this, I become hyper-emotional, to the point where I sometimes miss things that are happening around me. That's why I didn't hear a word of the introduction given by Janus to the crowd of party-goers who are now staring up at me.

I only hear one word: "PRIDEZILLA!" that echoes throughout the room as I make my grand entrance.

"Hello, Philadelphia! Hello Kensington! Hello to all you beautiful people. It's my honor to be here to entertain you tonight."

Music begins playing in the background, noticeable, but not intrusive.

"Is there anyone out there who remembers 1983?"

A few guys holler out their approval.

"That was over 40 years ago! And you guys are still out here partying? I am fucking impressed with y'all!"

There's laughter in the crowd.

"I only know 1983 from old videos. Let me start by taking you back to a magical moment, from 1983, in a place not too far from here, Central Park in New York City. You know Central Park, right? I've watched this lady perform this song at least a thousand times, and I still get tears in my eyes, just like she did, performing in front of 800,000 fans, so here she is, here I am, performing this, especially for you...and you...and you!"

I point directly to people below me and start my version of "Endless Love," written by Lionel Richie and originally sung as a duet by Richie and the incomparable Diana Ross.

I'm wearing my best Diana wig, long, curly, flowing, with a sparkling, long, white evening gown. I add my own fashion style, my own movements, and my personality to perform the song as a tribute. Not an imitation, but an appreciation. An homage.

Serving my best Diana to this young crowd, I see and feel their love. Thankfully, the tips are strong for this performance, while I transition into the second song, another hit from Diana, "I'm Coming Out," always a crowd favorite.

At the end of the song, the stage lights are turned off, leaving the stage awash in black light. My gown, which had fluorescent materials sewn onto the fabric, now screams in brilliant pink letters: *I'M CUM-MING OUT.*

That brings a roar from the crowd. Now I'm in my bag, unstoppable, entirely in the moment. The floor under me is littered with cash.

Act Two of my performance is a tribute to one of the finest superstars in the universe - Beyoncé. Without time for a full costume change, the black lights are extinguished, transforming my white gown back to its more natural state. It only takes a moment passing in back of the stage curtain to switch from my Diana wig to one more suited for this next act. Pulling on a pair of matching white opera gloves, to add a touch of glamour and sophistication, I call out:

"Where all my single ladies at? Make some noi-oise!"

"Come on, Philly, let me hear it! Single ladies? Any single ladies here?"

The crowd cheers as I begin belting out the mega-hit "Single Ladies (Put a Ring on it)," which is now a classic.

Philly is embracing me, my style, my show, and I'm feeling the love tonight.

Performing my second number by Queen Bey, from Renaissance, another beautiful song, "Alien Superstar." These lyrics mean so much to me, and I share my emotions with the audience, connecting with them.

Philly loves us Black Queens, I see, as I gratefully acknowledge the ovations and the tips.

While I feel inspired by the work of the artists who made hits of these songs, I don't pretend that I resemble them physically. At least, certainly not Diana Ross or Beyoncé.

That's why my set includes a tribute to a fat gurl like me. A fat, Black gurl like me.

You know who I'm talking about. One of the greatest ever. Lizzo.

For Part Three, I transform my look right on stage, in full view. First, off with the gloves. Next, off with the dress, leaving me clad only in a pink teddy, garter belt, and the sexiest pink stockings you've ever seen. Stepping out of my shoes, I then step right into a pair of bright red stiletto heels.

I'm greeted with waves of approving shrieks and screams when I sing "Good as Hell," a totally badass song. Naturally, I can't resist tossing my hair and checking my nails while I'm performing this hit.

Adding a song I hope will be a surprise, I lip sync to Lizzo's lovely rendition of "Pink" from *Barbie the Album*.

The audience cheers as I take my bow, but once more, I want to do the unexpected, as the DJ blasts one more soundtrack through the club.

Still clad in my pink lingerie, I add a pair of neon pink gloves and dark sunglasses, just like Ryan Gosling wore during his unbelievably entertaining performance of "I'm Just Ken," also featuring Mark Ronson, Slash and the Kens at the 2024 Oscars. What fun I have lip-syncing to Ryan's perfect rendition, but at the very end, I add my own spin to the lyrics.

The DJ remixed the song, so at the end, when Gosling sings that final line, it echoes through the speakers several times. And this is where I add my personal touch, changing the lyrics to suit me and this occasion.

In my own voice, drawing every bit of energy from the depths of my soul, I sing with more enthusiasm and passion than ever. I want the audience to feel me. To identify with me. And every single person, I believe, can and will identify, because none of us are perfect, plastic people. And so I wail:

"I'm Not Ken!"

"I'm Not Ken!"

"I'm Not Ken!"

"I'm Not Ken!"

My body is shaking with emotion as I let out a guttural scream at the climax of my act:

"Iiiii'mmm

Noooooooooot

Keeeeeeee-eennnnn!"

Then, taking my bow, I feel and accept every bit of the love and adoration aimed in my direction. I know in my heart that I made an impression, a damn good impression, on this crowd.

The Snark Sharks' regular members, Ru-Barb and Miss Dee-Eyed, had been joined by Marry Posa, aka The Butterfly, during Pridezilla's debut. Not a word had been uttered during the performance.

As Pridezilla exits, Ru-Barb was heard to say, "That...that was something else. That gurl actually got what it takes. I like her, no, I love her!"

To which Marry Posa retorts, "I think she was off by a half note at the end of that last song," bringing all three to fits of laughter.

"Child, you wouldn't recognize a half note if it jumped up and bit you on that Brazilian Butt Lift of yours!" screams Miss Dee. "Give a gurl a break. She put on one helluva show tonight and props to her!"

Facing myself in the mirror back in the tiny dressing room, I like what I see. An entertainer. An artist. A singer/dancer/comedian. I'm all that and more.

Though some might consider this vanity, I call it recognizing and appreciating my own talents. Having self-confidence and self-esteem are good qualities.

Janus knocks on the door and enters. "Jalen, first, totally awesome show tonight. Quick question. For the next two weeks, we're having a special Drag Wars event. I want to invite you to be in Group 2. You in?"

"Yes, darlin'. I'm in. I'm gonna knock 'em dead."

Janus leaves to announce the lineup to the audience. I sit back in my chair, smiling with satisfaction. I feel at home here in Philly. That's a good way to feel.

ROGUES' GALLERY

Taking advantage of opened doors, I find myself sipping champagne at Namon's Art Boutique, for the grand opening of his new exhibit, "DRAGGED," one of the cultural highlights of the Philly art scene. Olde City is famous for historical buildings, excellent restaurants, boutique shops and of course, art galleries.

Namon's is among the very finest. With Mateo at my side, and my glamorous outfit to hide the scared child from the ghetto inside me, I greet the art world bravely.

The exhibit features Drag Queens, of course. I'm struck by the many faces of drag, as captured on film by world-famous photographers. Style. Beauty. Grace. Humor. Sexiness. Fashion. And of course, gender confusion and non-conformity.

Strolling along, we see the themes in each grouping. First, I'm mostly amused by the Pop Star section. Seeing a photo of Troye Sivan in his alter-ego form embraced during his video for "One of Your Girls" brings to mind my...our...night at Díner en Blanc.

"I love seeing how they played with gender; I think they helped move the art of drag into a semblance of respectability," Mateo tells me, as we view Iggy Pop, Lady Gaga, The New York Dolls, Freddy Mercury, David Bowie and more, exuding sensuality and sexuality as they posed provocatively.

"Respectability, yes, but with a bit of rebellion thrown in for good measure," I add. "If we become too mainstream, we become boring, everyday creatures."

"You're so right about that," Mateo agrees.

Inside, I'm smiling at the comment I made. I've been practicing by listening to a YouTube show called *Talk Like a Gringo aka Speak Gooder English*. It's a funny title, which is what drew me to it, but I do want to sound more professional and I think it's helping.

"Look at all these Latinas!" I gush, as we come upon the next grouping. Bianca del Rio, the first Queen of Latin descent to win *Drag Race*, is featured. "She inspired me when I saw her on the show, oh my god, she's my Queen," I whisper.

"Look, there's Carmen Carrera, Adore Delano, and Roxxxy Andrews, too!" Mateo says, pointing them out.

It's no surprise that Mateo recognizes these stars. Everyone watches *RuPaul's Drag Race* religiously. We've been addicted for years now. It's a quality show, with the most fabulous host in the universe, and it now has spin-offs with Queens from countries around the world.

There's so much to see. Sections for Drag Throughout History, Drag Kings, Black Drag, all featuring photos that are intriguingly beautiful, with an air of mystery and mischief. At least, that's my interpretation.

At the very center of the exhibit is a masterwork of the Queen herself. A huge photo dominates one entire wall, with the simple title "qu33n."

It's Ru, of course, the person most responsible for bringing drag into public consciousness. Winner of multiple Emmy awards, she is perhaps the most funny, sophisticated, opinionated and knowledge-able Queen in herstory.

The photo combines three images of Ru. In the center, larger than life, she presents herself as the star of her show. Impossibly beautiful, flawless, dressed to perfection—the epitome of drag in style.

On the lower left is an image of a much younger, less-polished version of herself. There's a hardness to her glare, as she's looking out at the world, perhaps daring the world to defy her, to place obstacles in her path. I see determination in those eyes.

And in the upper right, a somewhat unexpected image. RuPaul, out of drag, looking as though he has accomplished his goals, bathed in satisfaction. Not in drag, but a Queen nevertheless. Because a Queen isn't defined by the clothes she wears, but by how she presents herself to the world.

Surrounding the main photo, there are 30 smaller images of Ru-Paul, the Queen of Drag herself, in a wide range of her manifestations. Bringing the total number of images to 33, hence the title of the piece.

I'm in awe at the work of the photographer, an original piece done by the gallery owner, Namon.

Immersed in the idea of the glory of drag, my thoughts are interrupted when I hear a loud, distinct voice close by.

I turn and see Divinity, looking very small and frail as she's standing next to what I perceive as a giant. A fat giant, no less. And she's a Queen! Oh my god, who is she?

Divinity approaches me quickly, after seeing that I finally notice her.

"Darling, let's put all that nastiness behind us, and let's be friends again," she coos, kissing the air near my face.

I don't have time to answer before she continues, "Let me introduce you to my new friend, Pridezilla. Pride, this is the infamous Fangula that I was telling you about."

"Oh, this Fangula?" Pridezilla asks, showing me one of my very own business cards.

"That's me," I tell her, while wondering how in the hell did she get her hands on that.

"Pridezilla is gonna be in the Drag Wars competition!" Divinity continues, again giving me no chance to ask Pridezilla about the card.

"Well, welcome to the contest, my dear!" I tell her.

"Thanks, I hope you and I will have a chance to get together sometime so I can hear your side of the story," the giant says to me.

My side of the story? My side? Now I know that Divinity has been spreading stories about me. I reach for my earrings, ready to take them off and hand them to Mateo before beating Divinity in an old-fashioned cat fight. I'm fully aware that the entire episode will be caught on video and will flood the Internet before we even get to the door. But maybe it's worth it. Some people claim that any publicity is good publicity.

"Donnie, you sure you wanna go there?" Mateo says softly. "Look at her nails. Sharp as knives. What if she cuts your face? Leaves a scar? Is that worth having a petty fight right now?"

Looking for an escape, Divinity tells Pridezilla, "Oh darling, there's Eliud. He has our drinks for us. Sorry we don't have more time to chat. Ta-ta!"

Divinity then whisks Pridezilla away from me, as if she's some sort of forbidden treasure. I didn't even have enough time to remove one earring before they're gone.

Mateo makes sure that the videographers and photographers catch our exit, just as every second of our entrance had been recorded, for posting on social media later. You know, the self-promotion game never ends.

I almost trip when we step out into the fresh evening air, perhaps having had one too many glasses of champagne.

"Next stop, the after party!" Mateo tells me, using his phone to summon an Uber.

That's when I see Slash, standing two doors down from the gallery. He's dressed in a much-too-large tee shirt, with the Fangula logo imprinted boldly on the front.

"Slash, what the...!"

"Just doing my little part to help your promotion," he tells me, winking, and handing my business card to both of us.

"You dawg! You really know how to do me good!" I exclaim.

Slash's face brightens. "I see you wore those shoes I bought for you. Damn, they is fine!"

He's right. Slash had spent a fortune buying me these Jimmy Choo pumps.

"And I see you're sportin' your new kicks, too!" I say, admiring the custom Jordans I had ordered just for him. "They look awesome."

"Thanks. I'm wearin' them to impress my date tonight. A new guy I met through my OnlyFans."

"Cool. Just be careful."

"Will do. No worries, darlin'. I'm always careful."

I love you," I tell Slash, kissing him on the cheek, just as the Uber arrives.

"I love you too, sweetness," he tells me, as Mateo and I drive off to the next party.

WAR BEGINS

The first night of Drag Wars is tonight, and instead of preparing for the show, I'm wasting my time at the 26th Police District on Girard Avenue, filling out the same form I've already given them during the past two days.

My hands shake as I take the form outside. I can't breathe in there. I need a smoke, something to calm my nerves. Just trying to get the cops to take me seriously is, at least up till now, an impossible task.

"Missing Persons Report" is at the top of the form, no more than a simple postcard. Last name, first name, middle initial. Date of birth. Address. Telephone. Email.

What are they going to do? Send him a fucking email to ask him where he is? I fume.

Height. Weight. Hair color. Eye color. Social Security Number. *How the fuck am I supposed to know that?*

Halfway through, my ballpoint pen runs out of ink, and I feel my patience oozing out of me as the last drop of ink oozes out of the pen.

Making a scene at the station isn't advisable, but I'm unable to control myself.

"I need to talk to someone right now!" I scream at the first person I find inside. "My friend is missing. Do you hear me? He's been missing for three days already. I need someone to help me, please!" I'm screaming, crying, terrified.

I get no sympathy. This isn't a TV show, where some caring cop drops everything to help the frightened young person who fears for her friend. This is Philly. The poor section. The place where dreams go to die. Everyone knows this and just accepts it. I don't know why I hoped for a different outcome.

It's the night of the show. My first drag competition, and getting ready for it has been a total bitch. It's been hard to concentrate with Slash still missing, but I have to go through with this.

I was counting on Slash to help me with the design and execution of my look for the night. He was always the one who created the overall look, even when we'd just pretend to do drag shows in one of our houses.

On top of that, Cobra hasn't come home yet, either. And every time I walk by Jamal's spot, the emptiness in my heart is as wide as the sky over the empty phone wires.

Luckily, Mateo has been doing his best to encourage me and cheer me on. At least one person is in my corner.

Arriving at the dressing room, Divinity and Claw!Dia are already there, having secured the "best seats" for working on their makeup. I'm prepared to breeze past them, but Divinity holds up her hand as if she's directing traffic, indicating that I should come to a full stop.

"Donnie, my dear, don't be like that," she says, placing one finger on her lower lip, then moving towards me while kissing the air. "Remember when we used to be friends? Do we want to let some guy come between us gals?"

"Isn't that what gals do?" I retort, though I instantly regret the remark.

"Wait. Hold up. Let me take that back," I offer, embracing the air around Divinity and returning the kisses.

"You're actually right. You got Elie now and I got my Mateo, so it's all good. Let's put that childish behavior behind us."

"Oh, you didn't hear? Elie already broke up with me. My heart is broken, so broken, I tell you. I'm not sure I can go on livin' without him."

All three of us burst out laughing at that, with Divinity laughing the loudest.

"Child, we know the game. Enjoy them, and then move the fuck on. Just like they do. We're too young to get all that serious about any one man, anyway."

Claw!Dia jumps in. "Damn straight. And we need to keep our sisterhood strong. If us Queens don't look out for each other, then who else is gonna do it?"

"Group hug, everybody," I call out, and the three of us, about to be competitors, enjoy a moment of solidarity. I won't lie; it was nice. As a matter of fact, that's exactly what I needed at that moment in time.

However, I've learned not to put too much trust in anyone. Not trying to sound negative, but I've been back-stabbed too many times to have full faith. That's just how it is, especially how it's always been for me.

Divinity, returning to her seat, pulls something out of her bag. "Look, gurl, I just got one of your tee shirts. Don't say I never did nothing to show my love."

Holding her Fangula tee shirt in front of her, I flash back to the night outside the art gallery, with Slash proudly wearing my merch.

"You heard about Slash going missing, right?" I ask Divinity.

"Oh god, yes, we're all worried sick about that boy. And I know how tight you two were. All my thoughts and prayers..." her voice trails off.

"Let's do this, ladies. Put all those worries out of your head, and let's make this the best show Fuego ever saw! And may the best Queen win!" Claw!Dia crows.

It's time to concentrate. She's right. I try to clear my mind, but it isn't easy to do.

I'm finally ready, just needing to slip into my heels when it's my turn to perform. With the door to the dressing room open, we listen as King Janus introduces the judges: Carlotta Sales, Harloweena and Midge. The crowd adores all three of them, each one a star in the Philly Drag community.

"We're adding a little to the pot tonight," I hear Janus announce. "Thanks to the size of tonight's crowd...and thank you all for paying that extra cover charge tonight...we're proud to say that the winner of tonight's semi-final event will receive a $500 cash award. And for the final event, the winner of the first Drag Wars event in Philly will receive not 1, but $2,000, along with claiming the Pink Tiara. The DRAG

WARS are now declared open. The battles will commence and may the best Queen win!

So with that, let's get the Queens out here. First up, please welcome our very own Divinity Thee Goddess!"

Divinity looks radiant, dressed in a satin kimono, with makeup and hair done Kabuki-style, as in the original meanings of the word: unorthodox and shocking. The dominant color of her makeup is red, signifying youth, justice, anger and bombastic strength.

Most of the meaning is lost on the audience, but that doesn't matter. They clearly love the overall look, based on the approving noise that greets her appearance.

Before the first notes of her music begin, the Snark Sharks are already circling, as if closing in on a fresh serving of sushi.

Ru-Barb set the tone: "My god, if she sings even one note of Madame Butterfly, I'm gonna throw a net over her and hook her myself!"

Nepharious: "I'll give it to her. That outfit slays. She looks better than any of the waitresses at the Japanese Tea Room."

Ru-Barb: "True, but tell me that kimono isn't on backwards. Am I wrong?"

"Nepharious: "Sshhh! Retract those claws, Miss Kitty! And yes, you're wrong. Where did you learn about Japanese culture? By watching Jerry Lewis in *The Geisha Boy*?"

Performing K-pop is a huge chance to take with this mostly Latino crowd from North Philly. But Divinity knows her people, her fans. And she herself is a huge fan of the genre. Besides, Divinity knows something most others don't. Midge, one of the judges, is a superfan of K-pop.

Her music is a mix of hits by both male and female artists. There's no rule that the songs have to be sung by females, and Divinity loves to break rules, even non-existent ones.

The mix is incredible, featuring samples from:

Take Over by Do Han Se

Stay Tonight by Chung Ha

Pretty Savage by BLACKPINK

High Heels by Brave Girls

The crowd adores her and every minute of the performance. Standing in the wings, I can see that Divinity is pleased not only with her performance, but with the reaction from the audience.

Once the noise quiets, Janus takes the mike.

"After the fiasco we had at a competition where we tried tallying the scores electronically, we're going back to the tried-and-true method of having the judges show their scores on their little broads...I mean, on their little boards. Midge, no offense intended. If you want to use a little broad, you have my permission to do so."

Midge is doubled-over with laughter.

"Any little broads out there want me to write my scores on them?" he shouts.

Janus continues, "The judges can choose a score of either 8, 9, or 10, based on presentation, performance and lip-syncing success or failure. We know that no one would ever deserve a score lower than 8, so fuck those other possible scores. Right, ladies?"

All the judges nod and laugh. This is a good time for everyone, as it's intended to be.

A scorekeeper, clad only in a red thong and red sneakers, hands a mike to Carlotta Sales, the first judge, then takes his place next to a whiteboard, where the scores will be tallied.

Janus turns to the boy, saying, "Honey, the highest possible score is 30. Do you have enough fingers and toes to count that high?"

The boy shrugs his shoulders. He knows his job is to entertain the audience by acting as if he isn't the sharpest crayon in the box.

The audience erupts in laughter.

"If not, I'm sure we can find at least ten dicks in the audience to help you keep score."

Again, the crowd screams in delight as Score Boy grabs his privates suggestively.

"All right, Carlotta. Let's hear it. Divinity is dying to know."

"Divinity, I loved the presentation and the choice of material. Your kimono is beautiful, but that tight costume makes it impossible for you to move with the music. My score for you this evening is a very strong 9."

There are groans from some members of the audience, but Divinity is gracious, folding her hands and bowing to Carlotta.

Janus says, "Score Boy, hello! Write the number 9 next to Divinity's name under the Carlotta column. What do they teach you boys in schools these days?"

Score Boy does as he's told, smiling and showing off his beautiful set of buns to the audience, one of the reasons he was chosen for this role tonight.

"Harloweena, you're up. What say you?" asks Janus.

"Divinity, you are a sight that sailors would cross the oceans for. That dress, that makeup, that hair. I am stunned by the absolute beauty. Your song selection was original. Even this old queen knew at least one of the songs. Or, at least, I think I knew one of the songs. And it's clear these young bucks and cucks in the audience know what it's all about. The one small drawback for me was the lip-syncing seemed just a bit off at a few points. I know it was a complicated mix, but you don't want to miss a beat when you're up here. I give you a very, very, very solid 9, my dear."

Divinity lets out a sigh, but quickly regains her composure, again bowing to the judge.

Score Boy does his thing, but first performs a few squats in front of the scoreboard, before reaching up to record the score. More than a few guys in the audience are paying close attention to his show.

"9 plus 9 equals what, Score Boy?"

"Help me out here, guys," Score Boy calls to his fans in the audience. He starts counting his fingers, "1, 2, 3..." and then continues by kicking off his shoes, "11, 12, 13..."

"If we ever get to 21, I wanna see that third leg of yours, boy!" Midge hollers out, grabbing hold of his crotch, waving his hidden junk at the crowd below.

"And speaking of junk, Midge is next," Janus laughs.

"Divinity, do not listen to these other judges, who clearly don't appreciate the beauty and brilliance of your work tonight. Without a doubt, my score for you is 10, 10, I'll say it again and put it up there, Score Boy. Write it as a 10!" Midge waves her board like a fan as she keeps shouting out the number 10.

"Boy, I'll save you the trouble," Janus says, not wanting Score Boy to count again. "Under the total column, write 28 for Divinity Thee Goddess. And with that, my dear Divinity, we thank you very much!"

As Divinity makes her way back to the dressing room, she gives me a wink and a thumbs-up. I wonder if I was wrong to doubt her intentions. However, I have other, more important things to think about right now.

The Snark Sharks are snarking.

Miss Dee Eyed: "Her lips barely moved. I thought we were watching a ventriloquism act."

Ru-Barb: "Yeah, but where was the dummy?"

Sandy Bichos (a new member of the Snarks): "Too bad her costume was so tight, she walked like the Mummy!"

Nepharious: "Calling Miss Blaine! Are you there, Miss Blaine?"

Ru-Barb: "I'm right over here, Antoine, my dear. And I think we can safely say that we..."

Ru and Nepharious together: "HATED IT!"

Claw!Dia is up next. Her banana print costume is reminiscent of Josephine Baker, but her song selection is pure disco, including "Physical" by Olivia Newton-John, "Girls Just Want to Have Fun" by Cyndi Lauper and "Dancing Queen" by ABBA.

Comments from the judges include:

Carlotta: "Love the music, but I don't see any connection with the costume. Am I missing something? A solid 9."

Harloweena: "I thought the same thing. Your lip-syncing is excellent, and I love your enthusiastic delivery. Good choreography, too. I'm happy to give you a score of 9."

Claw!Dia is hoping for a tie with Divinity, if she can just get the last judge to give a perfect score of 10.

Midge: "Gurl, I'd wear that dress if I could get it in my size. You know I love me some bananas! It's beautiful, exotic really. But where were the songs to go with the outfit? I wish the performance had been more coordinated. It could have been perfect. But it wasn't quite there. My score is 9."

Janus jumps in as Claw!Dia exits the stage.

"Score Boy! That's a 27 for Miss Claw!Dia."

Score Boy does his job, which is not only to record the scores, but to entertain the audience. Reaching deep into the extra-long pouch of his thong, he pulls out a marker, then proceeds to mimic oral sex with it, licking it up and down, sucking it hard, before finally recording the score.

Janus jokes, "Oh baby, I'll see you backstage after the show. I wanna get some of what you're givin'! And be sure to bring your banana with you, babe! Daddy here got some needs tonight!"

"Midge adds, "Can I be the second banana after the show? Puh-leeeze?"

My main thoughts as I prepare to go onstage are: *This Shakira wig weighs a fuckin' ton. I hope it doesn't fly off when I'm doing my head shakes.*

What a silly thing to be thinking, right?

My second thought is: *Without Slash or Cobra to help, I had to keep the costume simple. I hope the judges won't hold that against me. This sparkling red minidress with no shoulders contrasts well with my synthetic jade accessories, accentuating my emerald eyes. The string of tiny green lights that I weaved throughout the strands of my wig add a beautiful touch. I hope that'll be good enough.*

Janus introduces me and I leap onto the stage, aiming to keep the energy level high and the flavor "salsalicious!

My act begins with a string of Latina hits.

I want to open strong, so I begin with "Watati" by Karol G., from *Barbie the Album*.

Two can play the Barbie game, I'm thinking, knowing that this Spanish hit will resonate with my audience.

When I see the audience dancing along with me, I know I've captured their hearts.

My second song, designed to keep my Latina flavor going, is "Mayores" by Becky G and Bad Bunny. This hit provides plenty of opportunities to show off my sexy dance moves.

Again, I feel the love and support from the crowd. I keep my attention on them, though I want to look at the judges to see their reactions. But I dare not look.

Then, I make my daring move. I make my way off stage, carefully going down the steps in my 5-inch stilettos, heading for the Snark Sharks. The music stops dramatically for a full 5 seconds, and then I begin to circle them, moving my arms like I'm doing the breaststroke in the community swimming pool.

The music takes a dramatic change in tone. My goal isn't to anger them or embarrass them, but I do want to get their attention. And send a message.

"Sharks Can't Sleep" by Tracy Bonham does send the right message, I think. It starts as a ballad and turns into a hard rock anthem about how to treat people.

I sing the song directly to the assembled Snark Sharks, and the crowd loves every minute of it.

Then, I dramatically return to the stage for my final number, one that's sure to delight everyone here. "Hips Don't Lie" by Shakira is done to perfection!

At the finish, I'm overwhelmed and confident. The crowd lets me know how much they loved the performance.

"Thank you, thank you, everybody!" I address the audience, after getting a mike from Score Boy.

"Please, let me say something. I want everyone here to know just how much this night means to me. And I do hope, I really do hope to win. But I have something very important to share with you."

The crowd quiets down, as Janus signals for them to be quiet.

I run to the back of the stage and grab a poster.

"Look here. Please look here. This is my friend and he's missing and I'm so frightened. Most of you already know him. You might know him as Whitey, or by his new name, Slash, but this man means the world to me. He's been gone and no one has seen him since he disappeared after being seen outside Namon's Art Boutique in Old City. Please, please look at this photo. Remember his face and help me find him, please, I am begging you!"

I become silent, my shoulders slumping, and Score Boy comes over and wraps his arms around me.

Janus adds, "You heard the lady. If anyone knows anything, let us know. We can keep all information confidential. Just help us find Slash, thank you!"

"And now for the judging," he continues.

Carlotta: "Bold. Fierce. Beautiful. Done to perfection. That outfit could be worn by Shakira herself! The girl Fangula gets a 10 from me."

Harloweena: "Fantastic! What a great, energetic performance. Excellent song selection, with choreography done to perfection. But my dear, I know why you wanted to do that little portion about the Sharks, but it wasn't necessary."

Scattered boos can be heard from the audience at that remark.

"My score for Fangula is a very strong 9."

Midge: "Let me begin by saying your set made me hungry for some pinchos! Maybe Score Boy can take me out to a good place for some of that Puerto Rican carné," she jokes.

"But seriously, now it's up to me. I'm used to the pressure," she continues. "Fangula, darling, what a performance. It had everything. Music and costumes are perfection. Delivery is fierce and fabulous. And gurl, you got more balls than any other Queen, facing down the Sharks directly. I gotta say, I loved, loved, loved it. From me, Fangula gets a score of 10 and is now the official winner of this round of Drag Wars, with a top score of 29."

"Oh, just one quick note about the song she sang to the Sharks," Midge adds. "Ladies, I hope that you can take it just as well as you can dish it. And that's hopefully the last word on that subject for tonight."

Thrilled doesn't begin to describe my feelings. I did it! I'm a winner, and everyone here knows it.

I try not to let the hurt inside me detract from this moment, but my victory is bittersweet. The truth is, I'd rather be in the crowd watching with Slash by my side than be up here on this stage, accepting the cash prize and the love of the crowd around me.

BROTHERS AND SISTERS

"Divinity, I'm so sorry you didn't win. Did that cuntess Fangula cheat you out of it?"

"No, Jalen. Thanks. I appreciate you saying that. But the truth is, she earned that win. Her act was fierce. And she read the house right, going full Latina, plus taking on those Snark Sharks. I wish I had thought of that. Genius idea!"

"So you're not mad?"

"I'm disappointed," she confides to me. "But angry? No, I can't be mad at someone for having a better performance."

Life with Divinity has been a delight. She's more than a friend. She's interested in the community. She's proactive. She fears no one and enjoys overcoming obstacles.

She is a true SHERO.

"Let me know if you want me to do anything to help you get ready. It'll be Friday before you know it, and you're facing some stiff competition."

"I still don't know all the local Queens, but I'm making progress," I assure her. "I just want to give the best goddamn performance of my life. I wanna get into the finals."

Like everyone, the first thing I do in the morning is check my messages. After my win in the first round of Drag Wars last night, my phone is flooded, the comments on my Instagram are endless and, of course, my Twitter timeline is fucked up, just like it always is, ever since that billionaire took over. Scrolling quickly through the messages, I see the one I want.

Mateo: "Congrats on your big win, Donnie! I saw the whole thing livestreamed. Meet me at LOVE Park at noon for lunch."

My reply: "See you there, babe!"

LOVE Park! Why does he want to meet me there? Oh my god, do you think he's gonna propose? That's the perfect IG spot for proposal pix. I've seen so many, but I never thought I'd get my proposal there. Mateo is so romantic! How does he even know my ring size? I saw him looking closely at my fingers the other day. That must be why. He was sizing me up!

As my mind races with all these thoughts, I know I have to hurry. It's getting close to noon already.

I dress casually, but not too casually, in case of a possible photo op. Mateo's casual dress surprises me, and the fact he's gnawing on a hot dog from one of the nearby food trucks makes me think that perhaps I'm mistaken about the purpose of this meeting.

"You want a dog?" he asks me as I join him on the park bench.

"Uhmmm, no, no thanks. I'm good," I reply, a bit coldly.

"Ok, let me get right to it, then. First, major congrats on your win last night. So awesome!"

"But..." I lead him on, knowing he has more to say.

"Look, babe. You're a star. And you're gonna be a much bigger star in the future. And that's great for you. I really am happy for you."

"And what does that mean for us?' I ask him, afraid to hear the answer, but knowing he'll tell me whether I ask or not.

"You shine bright. Too bright. That shine casts a long shadow. And I have to be honest with you, I'm a man who doesn't want to be in anyone else's shadow. I want to be the star. No, check that. I need to be the goddamn star. I don't want anybody ever calling me Mister Fangula. That shit don't sit right with me."

I'm fuming.

"You mean to tell me I'm too fuckin' fabulous and you're scared to be overshadowed?"

"That isn't how I'd phrase it, but let's just say I'm not taking the backseat. I'm gonna be the driver. And that won't be possible with you. You're gonna be in one limo and I'm gonna be in a different one, with a beautiful, but quiet, bitch sitting in her place next to me. Not in front of me. Not pulling the strings. That's my place. The man's place. Case closed."

"Goddamn you and your fucked-up macho attitude. Go on with your pretty, petty self. If you can't appreciate a gurl like me, then you ain't deserve me."

I storm off, furious at him.

On my way home, I'm glad that I didn't tell anyone that I had been expecting to get engaged to that asshole. The only one I would've told anyway would have been Slash, still nowhere to be found.

Sometimes, just when you think a day can't get any worse, fate finds a way to push you down even more. Still angry at Mateo, I arrive home to find a notice from the Post Office for a package pick-up. I'm off work for the day, so I head over to the Post Office on Frankford Avenue, then stand impatiently in line to retrieve my...I don't know what I'm waiting for. The notice doesn't have any information about the sender.

I notice the young man leaning against the counter, staring at me. He doesn't look threatening, so I smile, which he returns.

"I saw your show last night," he calls out. "Loved it. You did a beautiful job and me and my friends had so much fun."

"Thanks so much. I'm happy to hear you liked it."

"When will you be back on stage? 'Cause I know I wanna be there, front and center."

"Not this Friday, but the next. I'll be in the finals of the competition. Don't know yet who I'll be up against."

"Let me know if you wanna go scope out the competition next week. I wouldn't mind being there with ya."

"Tell ya what, babe," I say to him. "Hit me up later this week. Today's been a bad day for me. Might not be the best day for me to be makin' plans."

"You got it, doll. Gimme your info and I'll hit you up later. I gotta go now anyways."

At the counter, I cringe when I see the package. But I sign for delivery and walk outside, barely able to breathe. It's Mami. They sent me her ashes through the fucking mail. I can barely hold onto the package with my trembling hands, so I put it down on the window sill of the building while I text Cobra.

Me: "Meet me at home, please. Right now. Important!"

Cobra: "Busy here."

Me: "No, you're not too busy for this. NOW!"

No reply from my brother, but when I get home, he's waiting for me outside.

Crying, I almost drop the package. Cobie helps me inside. He might be in a rebellious stage right now, but he is my family and we still love each other—at least, I think so.

"Want me to open it, or are we just gonna stare at it all day?" he asks me after a minute inside.

"Look, Cobie, we both know nothing's gonna change whether that box stays closed or gets opened. Go ahead, do it. I don't wanna be the one to do it is all I'm sayin'."

Inside the cardboard package is a plain wooden box. No urn. Of course not, we didn't buy an urn for her.

I'm thinking, but I don't know what to do or say, so I sit quietly, about to cry. I just feel...lost.

"Come here," he tells me, wrapping his arms around my shoulders. It's his turn to be the strong one, I guess.

And then he speaks.

"Mami, you're back home now. You're here with your family, your kids. And no matter what happened, no matter how much you were hurt, we get it. We understand. We forgive. But know one thing,

Mami. We ain't never ever gonna forget you. And now I just pray that you will rest in peace and in power."

I never loved my brother more than right now.

THE TALK

"**C**an we talk?"

"Who is this, Joan Rivers?" I text back, kiddingly. Of course, I know the text is from Bobby.

"LOL! But seriously, can we talk? Let's meet and spend the day together. You can even dress up as Joan, if you like," he texts back.

"Sure, let's do it. Where should I meet you?"

Though I chose not to dress as Joan, there's never any mistaking me for anyone other than a Queen. I don't have to be in drag. I carry myself majestically, and my royal aura shines for all to see.

Today, I'm sporting a wide-brimmed, floppy sun hat, sunglasses with huge rims covered in rhinestones, a flowery blouse, casual blue slacks, and low-heeled, pointy-tipped women's shoes. I don't spend hours shopping for shoes in my nearly impossible-to-find size just to leave them sitting home in a closet.

No wig, I'm not going all out today. But I wouldn't dream of taking a step outside without proper makeup. I'm not shy. I look good after applying my face. Plus, it makes me feel oh so fabulous!

Smiling as I approach Bobby, I appreciate that he isn't dressed for Casual Friday. His light blue seersucker suit, paired with a blue and yellow checked tie, screams the word "gentleman" at me. His sporty fedora and walking stick make the picture perfect.

"Let's play a game," he offers, as we walk along Walnut Street. "Three truths and a lie. You know the game, right?"

"Sure," I answer. "Who should go first?"

"Oh, I'm ready right now," Bobby says. "Listen up."

"One: I've never gone to a nude beach.

Two: Bananas are my favorite fruit.

Three: I'm a self-published author.

Four: I think I love you."

Talk about a twist to the game. What the hell is he thinking, with statement number four? I don't know if I should consider that as the truth or a lie.

"Well, lemme think about this for a minute," I tell Bobby. "For the first one, I don't know. Maybe you went to that famous nude beach up in North Jersey. Otherwise, I don't know of any around here. Then again, maybe you've traveled a lot."

"This is what makes it a fun game," Bobby replies. "See how well we know each other which, in our case, is hardly at all."

"Two has to be true. I already seen you eating bananas. Big, long, hard, wet ones, but still..." We both laugh.

"Three, again, I have no idea. You work in a library, so you love books. Maybe you wrote one, or even more. I'm gonna have to guess."

"Come on, tell me what you think!"

"Okay, I'm pretty sure that Numbers two and three are true. And I'm guessing you're flirting with me right now, so I'm gonna take a chance and say Number 4 is true, too. That leaves Number One, that you never went to a nude beach, as the lie."

I watch as he's smiling, starting to laugh, enjoying the game.

"I could say I cheated, and they're all true, or they're all lies," he teases.

"No, that isn't fair!"

"Okay, babe. I didn't cheat. And you are correct. Number one is the lie. I have been to nude beaches, more than one, and someday, I hope we'll go to one together."

"That means you think you love me, right?"

"Yes, I do think so. I hope that I'm not coming off too strong, too soon. I don't want to scare you off."

"No, Bobby. Not too strong. Not too soon. It's sweet and nice. But if I'm not ready to say it back yet, I hope I don't scare you off. Plus, you're only saying you think you love me, not that you're certain of it."

Bobby grips my hand tightly, smiles, and says, "No Jalen, I'm not one to be scared off easily."

"So, tell me about these books of yours. What do you write? Poetry?"

After the party celebrating the art exhibit, Mateo takes me home, like he does whenever he has early appointments the next day. Sitting in my room, I gaze at my version of the Drag Art show. Nothing like the one at the gallery, of course, but I do have a little tribute on my walls to Queens that I love. I like to cut the photos out of magazines, and I just use scotch tape to hang them. Others might find that sad and pathetic. Maybe it is. But that's all I can afford to do right now.

I have a special love for my Latine sisters in drag, so those are the ones I feature on my own personal Wall of Fame. Front and center is Bianca Del Rio; she's my idol. Surrounding her is what I call her Queen's Court, featuring other stars such as Crystal Methyd, Valentina, Monica Beverly Hillz, Poison Waters and of course, Salina EsTitties. Just looking at them, so glamorous, makes me smile.

I'm happy to fall asleep in such glorious company.

Waking up to silence, I'm a little concerned. Usually, I can hear Cobra bustling about in the kitchen, preparing breakfast. What he now calls our "cornflay." He can be so funny. But things are changing. He isn't here every day like he used to be.

Of course, I hope to be able to get us out of this neighborhood soon. I know he's vulnerable here, to outside forces like the local gangs, the dealers, even the sexual predators. I know he's already sexually active, but I won't let anyone hurt or abuse him. Not on my watch!

There's no sign of him when I enter the kitchen. Nothing's been prepared. No jokes being told. No smiling face to greet me.

I make a quick cup of coffee before heading out the door. My guess is he's spending time over at his boyfriend's house.

This is what I get, trying to raise a Queenager, I think, as the front door of the house slams shut behind me.

I take my usual shortcut, though I'm headed to Navi's place, not Slash's. They both live on the same block. When I reach that one special spot, I start to make the Sign of the Cross, in memory of Jamal, when I stop in shock. There are no shoes up there.

My mind blanks. *Am I in the right spot? Of course I am.* This is the exact place where I always, always, always take a brief moment of my day to remember my friend from school.

I don't remember any storm from last night, thinking that maybe the wind had loosened the strings, dropping the kicks to the ground. I'm looking, scanning the entire area, my eyes sweeping the street and the sidewalks for any sign of the kicks.

Nothing.

There's nothing here. Not even a friendly cardinal to greet me, hoping for a gift of a few sunflower seeds. Even Rojo is gone. Did he fly off with his family when he realized that he no longer had to safeguard Jamal's old kicks?

What words did I hear Jamal say the last time I was here?

I have to go back now, back to my safe place. Don't worry about me, Donnie. I'm good now.

Returning to his safe place. Is he gone forever now? Will this spot, that I consider to be sacred ground, just fall victim to the decay of this rotten neighborhood?

And how did his shoes just disappear overnight? It could be a sign, a warning that a gang war is about to start up again. Somebody might've stolen them just to start trouble between the gangs. Old loyalties don't just fade away and die. Not in Kensington.

If not that, what other explanation could there possibly be?

"This is a violation of the rules of this 'hood. Somebody's gonna pay for this," I mutter, as I continue on my trek to Navi's house.

I shouldn't be surprised by what I see when Navi's brother takes me into their living room. But I am. There's Cobra, slouched on the sofa, wearing, well...I've done enough web searches to know what you'll find under the search term "slutty school girl costume" on Google or Amazon.

Yes, the pink and black plaid super-miniskirt, the white blouse pulled up to expose the tummy, with the blouse's hem tied in a knot just below where a woman's breasts would be, and the white stockings with the little pink bows at the top hem.

I try not to look surprised, but my acting abilities aren't that strong.

"Aren't you supposed to be getting ready for school?" I demand, choosing not to mention the outfit. Not yet.

"Donnie, I stopped going to school two weeks ago," Cobie slurs. "Ever since I took my new name. I thought I was gonna earn some respect, but you know what the boys at school call me now?"

I wasn't sure I wanted to know the answer. I had been the subject of torment from too many kids at school to criticize Cobra for not wanting to put up with it.

"Crapola!" he hollers, his face contorting with rage at the thought. "Cobra Crapola! Oh my fucking god, do you think that's what I want the guys to think of me? Do you? DO YOU?"

I start towards my brother, but Navi steps in front of me, blocking my path.

"Donnie, it's time for you to let your brother go. He's mine now. I want him. I wanna take care of him. He don't need no school. He's gonna do just fine, you'll see."

"Is that what you want, Cobie? You want me to leave you here?" I call past Navi, who is not only blocking my vision, but seems to want to block my voice as well.

"Yeah, Donne. Go on home. You got your guy now. Let me have mine. I need a *caco* in my life. I'm gonna stay here with Navi."

Suddenly, Cobra's head slumps forward and his eyes roll to the back of his head. The truth slams me like a cinder block. *He's going down the same path as Mami. What in the hell am I supposed to do now?*

Dejected, I head home. Rejected by my own brother. Not that I can blame him. It would be hypocritical to lecture him for what he's doing since I did pretty much the same thing. He's dropping out. I never even made it to high school. Cobie already has more formal education than I do. He's leaving home. I left home at about the same age.

But I thought things would be different with us. I know why I left Mami's house. I thought that if I raised him, he'd feel more comfortable and secure, and then he'd follow a different path than I did.

But the pull of the ghetto is strong. I wonder if I have the strength to ever pull him back out of there.

One final look for Jamal's kicks as I pass the one spot in Philly that's sacred to me. No sneaks in sight. No bright red bird to comfort the hurt in my eyes and in my heart, as I mourn my old friend.

I glance over at Slash's house, and the thought of him outside the gallery last night gives me my first smile of the day. His blinds are still drawn, so I figure he's sleeping in. I don't want to bother him, so I go home to get ready for work.

I have a lot to do. Since I have some time before work, I check out my website and see that a few tee shirts have been sold. Slash did a beautiful job on the site.

Now I need to start working on my costume for Drag Wars. I know I can count on Slash to help me with the details, and I can do the basic design. I wonder if Cobra will do anything to help me? For once, I'm not sure about his support. I didn't realize just how much I needed him. Funny, I used to think that he needed me.

SHARKS!

Tuesday afternoon and I'm bored at home. Off of work, so how do I fill this free time? Nobody's around. Mateo's gone. Cobra's gone. Slash is gone, too.

I get a notification on my phone. Looking, I see it's a dick pic from Luisito, the guy from the Post Office. At first, I'm annoyed, but then I take another look.

Hmmmm, that is a nice one. Just the way I like them. Long, thick, uncut and juicy-looking.

Ok, I'm interested, but not at this very moment.

I text back a bee emoji, meaning I'm busy.

No reply right away. And then, the conversation continues:

●●●○○ Sprint LTE   4:08 PM   75% 🔋

< Messages   **Luisito**   Details

Does that mean you BEE
thinkin about me?

Or do that mean you
wanna BEE my gurl?

U too funny. It means I
BEE busy right now

Oh, oh, oh. But still, you
ain't said no. So you like
what you seen?

It's ok. I seen better

No, you ain't seen better
than mine. Stop playin
with me

The Crown Jewels isn't one of my regular hangout spots, but I head into Center City because I know that Ru-Barb will be performing tonight. She plays piano and sings old show tunes for an adoring crowd of 30 to 40 older gay gentlemen. They love to drink, they love the tunes, and they love Ru-Barb.

For them, it's about the company, the camaraderie. I understand, because I'm also feeling lonely this Tuesday night. The front bar is empty, but I can hear the joy coming from the back room as soon as I enter. I order a drink in the front.

I almost drop my Cosmo when I first step into the back, when the music stops and Ru-Barb's voice booms out. "Well, well, well, my pixies. Look who just dropped by. It's the one and only FAN-GHOUL-A!"

Everyone turns and stares, and then the funniest thing happens. Every single person in the bar turns their attention back to Ru, who picks up mid-tune, exactly where she had left off.

In their world, I don't exist.

They've never seen my website. They certainly aren't the type to take the trek to Fuego for a show. Instagram? Highly doubtful. Most of them look to be in their...I don't know...60s? 70s? Older?

And yet, they're having more fun than I am this Tuesday night. And Ru-Barb revels in it. She has her fan base. She has a place to perform regularly. And she's been doing this for the last 40 fucking years. A gurl could only hope to be that lucky.

Off to the side, not feeling comfortable enough to join the group, I watch how Ru interacts with her fans. Someday, I want to experience that kind of loyalty from a core group of followers. Hopefully, soon.

"Come over here and join me, darling," she calls to me, patting the side of the bench. I'm not one to hesitate about being in the spotlight, even if it's shared, so I scurry to her side.

Ru-Barb does her "Night of Cabaret" show in total drag, of course. Luckily, I'm dressed for the occasion.

"Do you know 'Not the Boy Next Door?'" she asks me, and I answer with a blank stare.

"You know, it's from *The Boy From Oz.*"

I feel like I'm from another planet right now.

"Ok," Ru continues, trying to find some common musical knowledge between us.

"How about 'Take Me or Leave Me' from *Rent*. Sound familiar?"

"Uhmmmm," I feel like a goddamn idiot. *What am I doing here, so far out of my element?*

Trying to lighten the mood, I ask, "Got anything from this century?"

Rather than answer, Ru-Barb says to her boys, "Intermission time, ladies. We'll take a short break. Fill up your glasses, and don't forget to fill up my tip jar!"

With that, she takes me by the arm, guiding me to a small booth at the back of the room.

"Ok, sweetie. Why are you really here? Ain't never seen you in here before and I know you ain't tryin' to have a duet with me. Whatsup?"

Sighing, I think for a moment before answering.

"I want to talk to you. I'm not sure what you thought about my performance the other night. And I don't want you to think I was trying to be mean or anything."

Laughing at that, Ru takes hold of my hand from across the table.

"First, Fangula, hmmm, is that what people call you? Fangula? It's a fabulous stage name, but can I ask, what do your friends call you?"

"I'm Donnie."

"As in Donald? Is that what your parents named you?"

"No," I laugh. "Even worse. They named me Adonis."

"Oh my god, they had no idea, did they? It's funny what parents expect of their kids. With that name, I know they weren't expectin' you to become the Queen that you are."

"Wait, it gets even worse. My middle name is Manlee. They named me Adonis Manlee Cruz."

We're both cackling like best friends.

"Child, let me tell you about how badly parents can mistake their child. You know me as Ru-Barb. But you know what my parents named me?"

"Let me guess. Rudolph, like the reindeer?"

"No. They named me Bob. That's my given name—Bob. Not Robert. Not even something kinda exotic, like Roberto. I have my birth certificate. It says it right there. Bob. The most plain, boring name for a guy in the English language. At least, that's what I think."

"So instead of boring old Bob, your parents got this pillar of fabulosity. You're right. They had no idea!"

It hadn't occurred to me that Ru-Barb could be anything other than a snarky shark. Yet here she is, sharing an intimate detail about herself, when she has no real reason to act sisterly.

"So, can I ask, what did you think of my performance?"

It was Ru's turn to take a moment to think.

"Gurl, when I see you, I see someone special. First thing I notice is your eyes. My god, that brilliant green color. If I was your parent, I would've named you Emerald. That would've fit you perfectly."

I'm blushing just a bit.

"And when you're on the stage, I say you have what we used to call 'IT.' Back in the day, you probably never even heard of her, but Clara Bow was the original IT Girl. You got that very same quality."

"Oh, you mean I got rizz."

"Rizz? I don't know what that means, honey. We used to say people had razzmatazz. You know, they stood out from others because of some special quality they had. It's always been hard to define, but people know it when they see it. Maybe now they call it the rizzmatizz," she laughs.

It's been a while since I had such a nice, pleasant, fun conversation.

"You're so funny!" I tell her.

"Can an old Queen like me give you a little advice?"

"Absolutely."

"You have the potential to be someone great. And you can and should choose your own path. But my advice is, along with your knowledge of today's trends and music, learn about some of your history. Learn about drag culture and those who came before you. And then honor those people. They struggled so that you...and even me...can do what we do."

"That's good advice. I'm definitely going to do that."

"And then, use your platform for something. Don't just be a pretty face, though you certainly have that. But grow beyond that."

"Any suggestions how?"

"Yes, as a matter of fact. First, don't do what I did. When I was just coming up, I thought of all the other Queens as adversaries, enemies. I tore them down every chance I had. And I did that in public and in private. I didn't recognize that we might play roles in public, even act as enemies, but it didn't have to be that way behind the scenes. They could have been my sisters. But I never gave any of them that chance."

"Wow! I do know what you mean. But it's hard to make friends."

"I'm not sayin' it'll be all lovey-dovey. Some will be interested; others might not be. But you can still make the effort."

I nod, thinking.

"And one more thing. In today's world, you can do a lot to be seen beyond the Philly drag scene. Maybe you can do a show on Ticks Tocks or something like that."

I pause, wondering whether to correct her.

"Gurl, that look on your face is too precious! Afraid to correct an old Queen like me? I know it's called TikTok. I might be old school, but that doesn't mean I don't know what's going on!"

"I can see you doing a show, maybe a podcast or something like that. Give it a cute name, like...I don't know...maybe *Dishin' It* or *Doin' the Dishin'* or something. You could have a segment where you dish on the Queens, then another segment where you tell your fans about some of the old drag stars from the past, and even do a cooking segment, like, makin' a dish. And that's just off the top of my head. Give it some thought, and you could come up with a brilliant format."

"*Dishin' It*...you know, I like that. I just might run with that idea. If I do, you'll come on as a guest, right?"

"Gurl, I would be honored."

"One more thing before I go," she continues. "It wouldn't hurt you to learn some of the old songs—the classics. There's a reason they're popular. Cause they're good. You even hear some of them come back in new shows. Like that song 'Running Up That Hill.' Everybody forgot about it till it was on that TV show. I forget the name of the show, but look it up."

"I heard that song, but I ain't know it was from a show," I answer.

"Now, let me get back to entertaining my boys. I'm the reason they're here tonight, you know. So they don't like me to keep them waiting too long."

I stand as if dismissed from class.

"I'm sure you got some nice young man waiting for you tonight. At least, I hope that's the case. Beauty like yours shouldn't be sittin' alone at home, not even on a Tuesday night. But keep in touch, child. Here's my number."

In return, I hand her my business card, after scrawling my cell number on the back.

As soon as I leave the club, I send a quick text to Luisito.

"Prepare yourself, babe. U are in for a major TREAT tonight. Your honeybee."

BATTLES WON AND LOST

"**W**hy do I get stuck with the Uber drivers who can't find their way around their own goddamn city?" I mutter to myself, approaching the club's dressing room, arriving later than I'd planned. The heel of my shoe decides to break at the very moment I'm turning the doorknob and pushing to get into the room.

The tiny shrieking sound I make as I struggle to catch my balance doesn't match the look of a tall, heavy Queen falling into the room, into the arms of an even taller Queen, who just happened to be standing at the right spot.

"Oh dearie! What happened? You okay?"

Her deep, throaty voice is like melted butter. Just what I need to help me calm my frazzled nerves.

"I'm Glamazon, the other contestant," she introduces herself. "And you must be Pridezilla. It's so nice to finally meet you! Though I didn't expect you to literally fall all over me," she says, laughing.

"Well, my Mama always said, be sure to make a good first impression!"

"Your Mama taught you good, then! Come on in and get properly settled. You know, you're not supposed to literally break a leg on the night of a show."

She's funny. I like her.

We both take seats at our dressing tables and work on transforming ourselves.

"Are you local?" I ask. "We haven't met before, but I'm still kinda new in town."

"Yeah, I live in Cherry Hill. Just across the river. You?"

"University City. I'm staying with Divinity right now. You know her?"

"Gurl, everybody knows Divinity. I love that girl. You're lucky to have her for a friend. She's a loyal one."

"You said you're the other contestant. I thought there would be three of us."

"Supposed to be. But it's just us. I heard the other gurl got arrested, hasn't made bail, and so she's out of the contest."

"Ohhh, I'm sorry to hear that. But we're here, so there isn't anything we can do about it, I guess."

Although we'd just met five minutes ago, we're chatting like we've been besties for years. I heard all about her boyfriend, her work as a beautician, and her home in Jersey, while I told her all about my Philly experiences, including Twiggy, Bobby, and the times I went to Drag

Queen Story Hours at the libraries. It's fun to see and hear what goes on behind the scenes instead of only knowing someone from their performances. It's a perk of being a fellow Drag performer.

Bobby sends me a text just as I'm about to text him.

"Best wishes, sweetness. I know you're gonna knock 'em dead. But remember, have fun. No reason to do it if you're not enjoying it."

"Thanks, babe," I text back. "Wish you could've made it tonight. I'll be thinking about you during the show."

"Love you!" is his simple reply.

Bobby doesn't tell me that he's already in the balcony, set to watch the show. He doesn't want to make me nervous about his presence.

"Judges, are you ready? Ladies, gents and creatures of the night, are you all ready?" Janus is a master at priming the crowd for the show.

"I know we're ready," snorts one of the Sharks to their assembled group. "If Glamazon comes out in a dress made out of Amazon packing tape, well, we'll just have to send her packing back to Jersey!"

"She couldn't possibly be any worse than that time we saw her at that fundraiser. Poor girl was so drunk, she didn't remember her lyrics and ended up flat on her ass right in the middle of the show."

"Oh, is drunk what they call it now? Nobody smelled any alcohol on that girl's breath. I tell you, she was so fuckin' high she's lucky her eyes ever came back to the front of her head."

Just before Janus introduces her, Glamazon pulls me over to her dressing table. "You want a quick hit?' she asks me, eyeing the white lines carefully placed on her table. "I don't mind sharing."

"Oh babe, thanks, but no thanks," I say, turning away.

It's an unfortunate reality that some entertainers, including Queens, use drugs, before, during and after performances.

They'll give all kinds of reasons. "It calms my nerves." Or, "I wanna have fun out there." Or, "It makes me a better performer."

I'm not here to judge. I can only decide for myself. That isn't my scene.

Glamazon does a couple quick hits, then shuffles to the door. Turning, she says, "Wish me luck, baby gurl!" and then she's off to perform.

Once I finish with my costume, I want to get a peek at Glamazon's show. Before I even get to the side of the stage, I spy a bundle of pure energy rushing towards the dressing room. I know I'm the only one who should be backstage, so I go back to check.

"Oh, hey there, I'm Lou. I got a last-minute message from Janus asking me to be in the show tonight, so I rushed right over. I got most of my makeup done while my husband was driving me over, but maybe you could help with my costume?"

"Ok, Lou. I'm Jalen, and I'll be happy to help. But first, you gotta fix that crooked lipstick and I think one of your eyelashes is on upside-down."

"Are you fucking kidding me? How could I have done that?" Lou looks flustered.

"No, babe, I was just kidding. Didn't mean to upset you. The makeup looks fabulous, and wow! You did that in a moving car? Color me IM with a capital PRESSED."

"Thanks, doll. This is a competition tonight, right? I hope I'm not asking too much by wanting some help with this costume."

"No, not at all. You're already at a disadvantage with no real time to prepare. So it's not a problem."

Straightening her wig, we're both listening as the judges voice their opinions to Glamazon.

Midge goes first: "Gurl, you're a fuckin' giant in this business and I always had great respect for you. But wow, babe, you were off tonight. That lip sync was like watching a foreign movie where the voice-dubbing machine is broken, and the lips don't even come close to matching the dialogue. I'm sorry, gurl. I did like your songs and you look like a rock star, but the performance didn't come together. I'm going out on a limb because you have a good rep, and my score for you is 9."

Carlotta: "This was a car wreck. Like, call the tow truck and get this mess outta here. I got mad respect for you, so Imma keep this short and just say the score is 8."

Harloweena: "Glam, Glam, Glam. You're one of my favorites. I still remember the first time I saw you, singing 'Glamorous Life' like you owned it. Damnit darling, where did that gurl disappear to? I know the crowd had fun with you, so I'm gonna go with them. They'd probably give you a 9, so I'll go with that."

Janus: "Score Boy! 9 plus 8 plus 9 equals...equals...equals...boy, we're waitin' on you!"

Score Boy stands there, shrugging his shoulders, then scratches his head, and then reaches into his jock pouch to scratch his balls. He knows how to have fun with the judges and with the audience.

"Boy, I'm about to knock you upside the head!" Janus shouts, barely able to contain his laughter. "If I made you count out the score with whacks from my paddle, I bet you'll get the answer right!"

Someone in the crowd shouts, "Paddle Boy!" Others join in, wanting more of a show.

Score Boy walks over to Janus, turns to face away from him, bending over, offering his butt to be used as a counting device.

"You asked for it, boy, so now you gonna get it!"

Twenty-six whacks later, his ass bright red, Score Boy walks over to write the correct score for Glamazon on the scoreboard. Glamazon has already returned to the dressing room, ready for another hit to dull the pain.

"You ready? Sorry about the last-minute notice," Janus checks with Lou before introducing her.

"Our next contestant for tonight is someone you're all familiar with. I know you love her as much as I do. Please welcome, straight outta Elkins Park, the one and only Miss Lou Seal Ballz!"

Before singing anything, Lou Seal pays tribute to the comedy icon she's been channeling for years, performing a comedy bit. She grabs Score Boy by the hand and pretends to be kissing him. Then she says to the crowd, "Knock Knock!"

The audience knows how to play along.

"Lou Sea, I'm ho-ome!" they sing-song.

With a shocked expression on her face, she turns to Score Boy and says, "Oh no, it's Ricky! He's home early. What are we going to do?"

Score Boy acts like he's cowering in fear, shaking next to Lou Sea, who pretends she's opening an invisible door.

That's what the crowd has been waiting for as they all scream, "Lou Sea, you got some 'splainin' to do!"

This delights the audience. Everyone knows and loves both the original Lucy and her devoteé Lou Seal Ballz.

Then her set begins, as she entertains with renditions of current pop hits, starting with "We Can't Be Friends (Wait for your Love)" by Ariana Grande, followed by "Dance the Night" by Dua Lipa and ending with "Snooze" by SZA.

Huge applause from the audience at the end, as Lou Sea gathers tips from many fans eager to touch her.

"Let's get to the judging," Janus announces.

Harloweena: "Gurl, what can I say? I love Lou Sea! You get a 10 from me!"

Carlotta: "Lou Sea, you got some 'splainin' to do! I'll never get tired of hearing that or seeing you perform. But..."

The crowd groans.

"But really, it's hard to be Lucy and Ariana at the same time. You know what I mean? I love the way you're doing songs from today, but it's a hard left turn from where your act starts. It's a little jarring. Now don't get me wrong, I love you to death, but for tonight, my score is a 9. A good 9. A great 9. But still, a 9."

Midge: "You are one helluva entertainer. You took hold of an icon and turned yourself into a version of her. I salute you for that. No one compares to you in that regard. But I do hear what Carlotta is saying. It's tricky to transform from a classic character into someone else right in front of an audience. You performed the songs brilliantly. But again, the disconnect is there. My score, my dear Lou Sea, is 9."

Janus: "Score Boy, do I need to whack your ass to get a total?"

"No SIR, I think I got this one figured out, Sir!" Score Boy screams, to the delight of all. Twenty-eight is the score for Lou Seal, two points ahead of Glamazon.

The Snark Sharks would like a word:

Ru-Barb: "I love Lou Seal to death, but tonight, she looked like Lucy in a flight attendant uniform. Maybe her songs should have been about airplanes, or flying, or something. Not whatever that collection of songs was. Could you even call it a collection?"

Nepharious sniffs: "I thought it looked more like a military uniform. She could have done some anti-war songs, maybe. I was sittin' here, waitin' for her to start marching around with a protest sign, or something. But lordy, I love when we get to tell her she's got some 'splainin' to do. The best part of the night for me!"

Sister Devil May Care, another semi-regular in attendance tonight: "The gurl was reaching. But she just couldn't catch it, ya know what I mean? When you end your act with 'Snooze,' you know you're gonna cause a few yawns in the house!"

"What about you, Auntie? Any thoughts?" Ru-Barb asks.

Auntie Histamine, known for her dry humor, states, "I'm just glad we didn't have to listen to the real Lucy singing, especially anything from *Mame*. Though that might have cleared up the congestion in my head!"

Reaching into her bag, Auntie pulls out a bottle of nasal spray and proceeds to take a couple whiffs.

Ru-Barb, sniffing loudly, says, "Not so much, Auntie dear. We don't wanna have to use the Narcan...again!"

Everyone laughs.

"Now, Barbie...may I call you Barbie?" Auntie sneers, casting a side-eye in Ru-Barb's direction. "Let's not be so personal. We all have a few skeletons in the closet, and I don't have to dig too deep to expose yours."

"Oh, hush, hush, sweet charlatan," Ru-Barb replies, her voice dripping with sarcasm. "Go ahead, sniff yourself to an early grave. Nobody here thinks you got saline spray in that little bottle. We know what's up. Now seriously, hush yourselves, all of you. Here comes the next act."

"All right, people, it's time for the final act of the night. She's new to our city, but already making a big impression, so let's make the lady feel welcome. Everything you've heard about her is true. Here she is, Pridezilla!"

I know how to act. I know how to sing. And I can be the sexiest mother in the house. So I take the stage with total confidence.

As instructed, Score Boy had wheeled out a large, high-backed, swivel leather chair from the club's office. I approached it stealthily, clad in black from head to toe, accented by my brilliant red lipstick, red eyelashes and red heels.

The costume is all leather, with a tight bodice, a miniskirt, and sleeves with twisted leather bands in the shape of barbed wires. My veil looks like a cobweb, which I clutch with my acrylic, sharply-pointed nails, done in a glossy finish.

My first song, "Disturbia" by Rihanna, is choreographed much like her video, a personal favorite of mine. I struggle and writhe against invisible forces holding me down, occasionally breaking free, only to be drawn back into my imprisonment on the chair.

Without skipping a beat, I move into my second song as Score Boy joins me on stage, wrapping a huge cape around me, adorned with a pattern of red and yellow flames. "Swirling, twirling, and kicking up a storm, I perform "Love the Way You Lie," by Eminem featuring Rihanna, but with a twist.

Score Boy stands still on the stage, his arms clasped around his body, as if to protect himself. I sing both parts of the song. When Eminem does his rap, I drop the cape to play his part, as Score Boy takes the simulated verbal and physical abuse from me. He actually gets so emotional during the performance that I can see the tears in his eyes. When I sing the Rihanna verses, I put the cape back on, until the end, when I throw the cape on top of Score Boy, pushing him to the ground, acting as if I'm spitting on him and kicking him.

The crowd reaction is wild. People are screaming and cheering. Inside, I'm glowing, while on the outside, I'm a raging fury.

At the end of that song, everything goes quiet for a few seconds. I'm a gurl who loves a dramatic pause.

Score Boy stands up from the floor, casting aside the cape that was covering him. From a hidden compartment in the cape, he grabs a straitjacket and approaches me, as the third song begins.

He's been instructed not to actually touch me during this song, but only to stand close by as I perform an emotionally wrenching version of "Rehab" by Amy Winehouse. The applause at the end tells me that the audience thinks the show is over, but I like to surprise everyone, so I allow Score Boy to fasten the straitjacket on me, making it impossible for me to move my arms. I sit back into the chair and perform my final number, a different song but with the same title. This time, it's "Rehab" as performed by Rihanna, in the video that also features Justin Timberlake. Throughout the number, Score Boy stands close by me, slightly off to the side. I sing the song to him, never moving my eyes away. The audience witnesses my struggle, an outward display of emotional turmoil.

At the end, my emotions are raw, and at this point, I can barely see the crowd, as my eyes are filling with tears. Score Boy wheels me off stage, still confined by the straitjacket, to thunderous applause.

Now, I prepare myself to hear the judges.

"Judges gonna judge, so let's hear it from our guests of honor!" King Janus announces.

Midge: "Pridezilla, my dear, I am stunned and amazed. What a goddamn talent you have. And grace and beauty completes the package. This was original, engaging, and gave me all the feels! Gurl, I am so proud to give you the first of what I hope will be three 10s for you tonight. You deserve it, babe. Write it down, Score Boy, 'fore I whup your ass!"

Harloweena: "Child, I am swept away. You're one helluva Rihanna, but oh my god, you did Eminem like a pro. Switchin' up to sing both roles was a move that marks you as a professional, a keeper, a star! And good job using the boy there as a prop. I enjoyed that part immensely. Boy, write down my score. It's a 10!"

Carlotta: "You hurt me tonight. You hurt my very soul. You touched me in places where even my husband cannot reach....and he got a major biggie, you know what I'm sayin'? Darling, this was one of the best acts ever. You deserve to move on to the finals. Boy, do your job and write down the score. That's a big ole One Zero, Ten, Ten, Ten!"

"May I say something?" I ask, with Janus nodding his permission. "Thank you very much, Judges, for the feedback. I'm in awe of each one of you. And to you," I say, sweeping my arms out to the crowd, "Thank you for welcoming this Queen with open arms. I love each and every one of you. And I'll be back for the finals next week, and I promise to give everything I've got to entertain you. Good night, my beauties!"

King Janus takes over the mike. "Listen up, Queers. The stage is now set for the final battle in Drag Wars. Don't miss it, next Friday.

Personally, I cannot wait to see this. It's gonna be epic. It's Fangula vs Pridezilla!"

LUCKY

Twenty-seven blocks from the spot where Jamal's kicks had been tossed over the phone wires, twelve-year-old Petey says to his dad, "I wonder if Lucky's ever gonna find her way home. It's been a month since she ran off. I know she's lost and trying to find her way back. I hope she isn't scared, especially in the night."

"I'm worried, too, Pete. She never ran off like that before. You wanna go ride around the neighborhood again, looking for her?"

Petey's dad continues, "If we find her, we'll have to start keeping her collar on her all the time, even in the house. If someone finds her now, they won't know where she belongs."

"I know," Petey answers. "But we never expected her to go running after Ms. Crawford's cat like that, when Lucky was just sittin' there by the door."

"Yeah, she took off like a rocket! And then I expect she just got lost and couldn't find her way back home."

"I was just thinking about the way she would always wanna grab your sneakers and run off to hide with them. I think that was the most fun thing for her in life. Chewing on your old sneakers. Isn't that funny, Dad?"

"We got another call about that stray who's been running around Kensington, knocking over trashcans and trying to steal food. Someone thinks they found her and her nest. I guess she was hunting for food to feed her pups. Let's go check it out."

Twenty minutes later, two volunteers from the Kensington Animal Shelter are watching that stray, huddling with her puppies, protecting them.

Holding out treats to lure the stray out of hiding, Jason tells Mikey, "Look at that. This girl found some old beat-up sneakers and it looks like she was using them to line her nest. Plus, it looks like she enjoys chewing on them, too. They're totally shredded."

"I see that, Jason, you're right. And look at the way the old girl has white paws, kinda like she's wearing sneakers, too. That's what we oughta call her. Sneakers."

"Yep," answers Mikey. "And look, there's a name written on the kicks. It says, 'Jam.' We can call one of the pups 'Jam,' maybe that little one that's chewing on the heel right now."

With Sneakers, Jam, and the rest of the pups safely in the back of the van, they drive back to the shelter. "Someone's gonna adopt these cuties for sure. I might even take one home myself," Mikey says.

SLASH

Four days later, as Fangula and Pridezilla prepare for the Drag Wars final battle, set for Friday at midnight, a text message is sent.

"We might have some info about your missing person. Can you report to the station? ASAP, please."

I stare at the phone, frightened. It doesn't say much, but it sounds bad. It doesn't say that Slash was found, and there's no mention of whether he's safe or not. I run out of the house and down the street.

When I get to the station, Slash's mom is already there. She looks weary, shoulders hunched, the thousand hurts of a lifetime etched into her once beautiful face.

"Oh, Donnie. Oh, Donnie. It's him. He's in there." She points towards a closed door.

He must be alive, I think. *Why else would he be here? If he had died, wouldn't they take his body somewhere else?*

There's an officer standing at the door. "We need a positive ID. His mother says that she can't look. But let me tell you before you go in, it's bad. I want you to be prepared."

I nod. I don't even feel my body as I step inside. All I hear is my breathing, like a monster, breathing so heavily that no other earthly sounds can penetrate.

Instinctively, I hold my folded hands at my mouth as the sheet is pulled back.

I am appalled. Can this be real? I stand still, utterly shocked, unable to comprehend this sight.

Slash's head is completely caved-in, his eye sockets empty, a bit of his mouth is twisted in agony. I reach for his hand, and the coldness turns my heart to ice, about to crack open in my chest and slice me open with a million slivers.

He's still soaking wet, having been pulled out of the Delaware River not long ago.

"It looks like he got dumped somewhere along the river banks, or maybe he slipped and fell. We don't know what happened yet."

I want to scream at the officer, but what good would that do? I want to tear the room to shreds, again, a useless, pointless act.

I hear a voice, but I don't understand the words. The voice says something again.

"Is that him? Is that Franklin Mayflower?"

"His name is Slash," I mumble. "His name is Slash. But yeah, that's him."

"Are you 100% certain?"

"Yes, look. He's wearing the shirt he wore that night at the art gallery. That's me on that shirt. I'm Fangula. I'd know that shirt anywhere. And look at his shoes. I bought those kicks for him. Those were his favorites. And look at his back. You'll see a tattoo back there. It'll look just like this one," I say, turning and showing the officer my tramp stamp.

"Even with the exact same initials in the center. So yeah, lady, I'm sure. I never been more fucking sure of anything in my whole god-damn life."

Before I leave, I turn to Slash. "Whoever did this, I'm gonna find him and I'm going to kill him. If it's the last thing I ever do. I promise you that, Slash, I promise you that!"

Outside, I hug his Mom to comfort her. She's been my second Mom forever. We spent so many hours at each other's houses, it was like we were all one big family.

"Ms. Mayflower, I'm sorry to have to ask this, but if I don't do this one very important thing, I might never get the chance to do it."

"What're you talkin' about, sweetie?"

"His kicks. I know it seems harsh right now, but I wanna do the right thing and honor him in the way we do. You know what I'm talkin' about, right? And I feel horrible askin' your permission, but if I don't take them right now, before the cops even notice, I won't ever be able to get them."

Slash's mom looks at me with profound sadness overtaking her.

"You're my family, just like my son was. You go in there and do what you gotta do. If anybody comes by the door, I'll distract them if I have to."

I wish I could erase the memory of that horrible moment in my life, when I went back in and removed Slash's sneakers from his feet.

They're dripping, and I can't leave a trail of water, so I slip them into my oversized Birkin bag. If the bag gets ruined, it's no big deal. I know where I can get a replacement at the market under the El for $29.99. But I'm not thinking about that. I have to get out of the station before anyone realizes what I'm doing.

A short time later, Cobra meets me in the alley.

It's hard to ignore his hair, now shorn very close to his scalp, dyed in stripes of red, white and blue.

I wonder what the hell that means, I think, without asking. I'm not in investigative mode. I have a ritual to perform. I'm so intent on my mission that I don't even comment about the horrid, bright yellow Crocs that he's wearing. I used to count on Cobra to help me with my costume designs. What's happening to him?

It's only been two hours since I was at the station, seeing my bestie for the last time ever. Some ceremonies cannot wait. I do not have the patience to gather folks together or to give a sermon about what Slash meant to me. I know that Slash heard it from me when he was alive. Nothing I say now will be heard by him. But still, I have to perform this final act of love.

I toss his kicks up, and they fall to the ground. Missed. I try again. Miss again.

"Want me to try?" Cobra asks.

"No, it's gotta be me. I gotta be the one to do it." And on the third try, the laces catch on the wire, wrapping themselves around a few times, leaving the sneakers swaying in the air.

Slash is now memorialized for the entire neighborhood to see, and though my heart will be forever broken, at least I could do this one final act of love for him.

Just as I'm about to walk away, a loud, fluttering sound and frantic chirps capture my attention. I feel my heart thumping in my chest as my little red friend, Rojo the cardinal, suddenly comes into view. All alone, no mate, no babies. I wonder why.

He recognizes me, flying in my direction, looking for seeds. But I have none today and I silently curse myself for not having faith.

I watch as he begins to dance. Gliding to the ground, then onto a nearby tree stump, then back to the same spot on the ground, into a clump of overgrown weeds. Chirping, more and more loudly, I begin to think that he's calling me.

"You got anything a bird might wanna eat?" I ask Cobra.

"Do they eat grass? Like, you know, our kinda grass?"

"Hell, I ain't know. Gimme some and we'll find out."

Rojo is still fluttering back and forth, from the ground to the stump, and then he flies around me, settling into the weeds, and once more jumping up on the tree.

Gingerly, I move forward, holding out the weed, which is all I have to offer. But Rojo pays me no mind, once more jumping into the grass and starts chirping, pecking at something.

I stop cold dead. My brother watches my shoulders heaving as an ungodly wail escapes from my throat.

"What in the name of Cheeses H Christ is it?" he asks.

Bending down, picking up a small piece of leather, I turn to show my brother. In my hand is a relic, which for me is holier than any relic in any church—a small bit of leather, with the letters "AL" scribbled in black Sharpie.

"It's Jamal! It's Jamal!" I'm about to fall to the ground, so Cobra rushes over to support me. Cradling this sacred little remnant, my heart finds just a bit of peace. Jamal is back with me, in the only way he can be. I have to be satisfied with that.

Once more, I make the Sign of the Cross, silently sending thanks to my little red friend, as I watch him fly off into the east.

"Be there in 20," is the reply I send to the message from the Medical Examiner's office, a little after 2:30 AM.

"It's gotta be news about Slash," I tell the Uber driver, who shows no interest and has no reply.

Running into that room, the one with those metallic sliding drawers where bodies are stored, I find myself alone. One body, covered by a sheet, lies on a nearby table. Unsure if I should wait for someone, I pause, then slowly approach the table.

Just like I've seen in a thousand horror movies, the body sits up, the sheet falls off his face, and Slash, his face distorted, destroyed, says to me, "People don't always deserve what they get, nor do they always get what they deserve."

My scream in the dream is loud enough to awaken me. The rest of the night is spent in despair. Not even sleep will be my companion tonight.

THE FINALS

Since Drag Wars is a competition, I put a lot of emphasis on preparing new material and costumes. Sometimes, it's perfectly okay to re-use costumes and routines for a show. But not this week. If I want to win, and I do, it has to be something out of the ordinary and definitely fierce and fabulous.

"What kinds of ideas do you have for Friday night?" Divinity asks me, as I prepare to go and meet Bobby and Ruby. I want to ask them for ideas and advice—especially Ruby, since I'm considering doing something campy and retro.

During our conversation, mostly focused on song choices, fabrics and accessories, the subject of drag in general comes up.

"Would you ever consider giving up drag? Or is this a lifetime commitment for you?" Bobby asks.

I don't have to stop and think. I already know the answer.

"Honey, drag isn't what I do. Drag is who I am. So, just to be clear, this Queen ain't gonna stop performin'. I might not always take the stage, but I can put on a show anywhere, anytime."

"That's what I thought. I'm glad you know that you're on the right path for you," Bobby answers, as Ruby nods approvingly.

"My brother Rudy never gave it up. He lived for show nights. I understand why. It was the most fun he had, entertaining the guys and just expressing himself. I really miss him," Ruby continues.

"Tell me about his act again, Ruby. You said he'd make himself up to look like Endora? She's an icon. Can we find some of her old photos from *Bewitched* online?"

"Look at these!" Ruby says, showing me the photos of Agnes Moorehead, looking like an outrageously campy Queen, on a show that was beloved by America.

"Even her outfits are so perfect. And that wig! Where can we find one of those?"

"I already have one. It belonged to Rudy and he adored wearing it as Rubee Red Lips. It's been in a case all these years. I better check to be sure it's still in good condition."

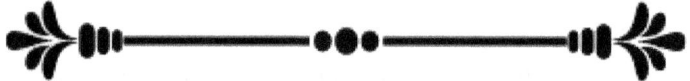

"Can you come over here and help me out? I got a show Friday."

Cobra texts me back. "Can't you get nobody else? Busy here."

"Please?" I reply.

Ten minutes later, Cobie's at the door.

"I need help with my costumes and I can't update my site. I need your help. I can't do all this."

Cobie nods.

"Ok, but can I ask you somethin' first? It's kinda weird."

"My middle name is Weird, babe. Tell me everything!"

"Well, it's Navi. He's actin' really weird. Yesterday he got me a new outfit. He ordered it from Amazon. I'm expectin' somethin' sexy, and he pulls out this big ass robe and a crazy-lookin' hat and tells me he wants me to be his handmaid."

"What the fuck's a handmaid?" I ask.

Cobie sighs. "He says he wants me to dress a bit modest. Those are his exact words. A bit modest. Who even talks like that? And then he tells me go put on this robe and hat, he called it a bonnet, and then come out of the bedroom so he can look."

"What happened then?"

"I'm tellin' ya, it's crazy. The night before, when I was wearin' somethin' sexy like a hot bitch, his dick stay soft the whole night. But when I put on this gown, he calls me a good, obedient girl, and I'm gonna be his handmaid and his dick springs up like crazy and he fucks me like a dawg. I told you it's weird. Whaddya think about that?"

"Did you like it?"

"Course I liked it. I got the dick. But I don't understand why he gets hot when I look like a plain Jane."

"Hmmmm. I don't know. Maybe it wasn't the look so much. Maybe it was that you was obeyin' him. You know guys, they like that shit."

"He told me we're gonna watch a show called *The Handmaid's Tale* startin' tonight, and the show is gonna learn me how to be a proper female for him."

"Ohhh, you a female now, huh?"

"You know I ain't. But he treats me like one. And now he's talkin' like gurls ain't supposed to have pleasure from sex, so he's gonna make me be denied my pleasure. This is so crazy!"

"Well, Cobra, if it gets too crazy, come back home. You ain't gotta stay with him, ya know."

"Yeah, I know—and one more thing. Navi said I can't be called Cobra no more. He says that's a dude's name. He told me my name is Cookie now."

"Cookie? You like that?"

"Kinda. I like he gives me a name that's special just for me. He said it's 'cause I'm sweet and he likes to eat me."

"Ok, Cookie. If that's what you want. Just remember, don't be afraid to come back home here if you ever wanna."

"Hey, that show you're watchin'. Do you know if it got any old songs in it? I'm lookin' for some new ideas for my act on Friday."

"Lemme check," he answers, searching YouTube for songs from *The Handmaid's Tale*.

Air kisses and embraces fill the tiny room as King Janus escorts me into the dressing area, where Pridezilla had arrived just moments before.

"Now, ladies, I know I can trust the two of you to behave. This is a big night for all of us, including the club. Lots of money to be made and a crown to be snatched by the one deemed most worthy."

"No problem from me, I promise," I tell Janus.

"Same from me. We hardly even know each other, so no feuds or nothin' between us."

"Not yet, anyways," I say with a smile to show I'm kidding. At least, mostly kidding.

"Now, I could tell you ladies that both of you are winners. And you are—semi-final winners. But only one Queen wears the crown tonight. I'll be placing the Pink Tiara on the head of the winner, no matter which one of you that is. But I wanna take a quick minute to say, I do love both of you. I can't even pick a fave. So both of you, go out there and slay it tonight!"

Left alone together for the first time ever, we feel each other out.

"So, you're with Divinity now. In her house. How's that workin' for ya?"

"I ain't gonna lie. It's good. She took me in when I needed help and I'm grateful to her. I know she can act tough, but that's true for all of us, right?"

"You got a point there, honey."

Time flies by as we again transform into our most magnificent selves. Queens. No one can take that title from us.

I feel my heart beating fast, listening to the crowd getting louder out there.

Snark Sharks are on patrol, eagerly awaiting this final round of Drag Wars, ready to shred anyone who shows fear. They respect ferocity because that's their source of pride. No one would ever describe those Queens as weak or timid.

Ru-Barb, as usual, leads the group: "I feel like we're about to witness the *Clash of the Titans* tonight. I hope they both remembered to wear their big gurl panties."

Glamazon has joined the group tonight, not wanting to appear defeated after last week's fiasco. "Honestly, ladies, I think the fix was in to get the two youngest gurls in the finals. I coulda been up there tonight, ya know."

Ru-Barb: "Honey, do you really think it's a good idea to mention the word 'fix?' 'Cause as I recall, you looked like you took a couple fixes right before your act last week."

That remark draws hoots and cackles from the rest of the Snark Sharks.

Mama Casa is with the Sharks this week. "I'm rootin' for the big gurl tonight. I hope she's good. We need more representation up in the house, if you ask me."

"Child, shut up and chew on that ham sammich, but don't choke," Glamazon says, winking at the others, knowing this triggers Mama.

"Don't you ever get tired of that same, lame joke? You know that was a rumor about Mama Cass, and now we all know it was never true," Mama shoots back.

"Not really darlin.' What's funny is funny, and that one ain't never goin' out of style," Glamazon snorts.

"Sshhh, here they come!"

The voice of King Janus echoes throughout the club, greeting the crowd, introducing the judges, and then the first contestant.

"Everybody in here knows her. Some of you know her very, very, very well. Or so I've been told. Personally, it's hard for me to believe that a face this beautiful would ever have anything to do with some of your nasty asses."

Groans and laughs are heard from the crowd.

"And here she is, the Fabulous, the Ferocious One, ready to pounce out of her lair. Please welcome the one and only Fangula!"

Although I'm walking alone out on the stage, I feel like I'm in a procession. My last procession was back at 8th Grade graduation from Roberto Clemente Middle School. My best friend Whitey walked behind me that day, making smart remarks the whole time about how I wiggled my ass when I walked. That day, he made me laugh. The thought of that memory today has me on the verge of tears.

Brush that aside, I remind myself. *I have to perform. Right now.*

My bright red robe swirls about me as I slowly make my way to center stage. My head is bowed, covered in a white bonnet. I am a Handmaid. The music begins.

"You Don't Own Me," a song I'd never heard until two days ago, opens my performance. Sung by Lesley Gore, it was a hit sometime in the 60s and then brought back into pop culture as a signature song in the series *The Handmaid's Tale*.

I can't see her, but I'm certain that Ru-Barb is smiling at this choice.

As the Lesley Gore song fades out, concluding her anthem about freedom, the music transitions to my second, perhaps riskier choice.

This requires a swift costume change, so I rush behind the curtain where Score Boy and Janus are waiting to help me out of my robe, fastening a set of massive black wings to my back.

My hands, now visible, are covered with claw-like gloves, featuring massive nails, pointed like spikes. In homage to Gaga, I call them my Chromatica claws, designed somewhat like those she wore during that tour.

I can manipulate the wings using small levers near my chest, which are invisible to the audience since they blend into the black fabric of my body-clinging catsuit.

Another song written long ago, but newly released by superstar Beyoncé on her new *Country Carter* album, I do a slow, sultry rendition of "Blackbiird," originally performed by The Beatles, and written by Lennon/McCartney as a tribute to the struggles of Black women during the Civil Rights Movement.

Knowing that the crowd and the judges will all expect a grand finale, the third song begins, and I expose the raw, tattered heart-broken wreck of myself onstage for all to see, performing "Unstoppable" by Sia. At certain parts of the song, I crouch low to make myself appear small, wrapping my wings tightly around me like a suit of armor, protecting myself from the world. But for most of the song, I'm proudly strutting, showing my pride and ferocity, clawing at the air as if I'm shredding an unseen enemy.

By the end, I'm screaming. I let my anger take over, tearing the wings from my body, stomping on them as if they're the cause of my pain.

The people at the costume shop won't like it when I return these broken wings, enters my mind, but just as quickly, I dismiss the thought. I can think about that later.

As the music ends, I turn to face the audience, my face red and contorted with anger, saying, "I know someone out there knows what happened to Slash. And I swear, I'm gonna find you and I'm gonna fuckin' kill you."

Those final words echo around the room, as if the DJ had it on a repeated blast. "Kill you, kill you, kill you."

Unsure what to do, since this had not been planned, I decide to act like nothing strange had just happened. I bow to the audience, blowing kisses, and walk around the stage, collecting tips.—lots and lots of tips.

Janus gives the crowd a moment to quiet down. The audience is buzzing about the performance, about Slash, and emotions are running high.

"The moment has arrived. Time to pass your judgment," he finally announces.

Carlotta: "I am stunned. I can't even feel myself right now. My emotions poured out of my body and they're still running around the stage, kinda like little miniature cars that ran off the track. Honey, what I'm trying to say is...tonight's performance was profound. A surprising mix of songs that told a story, a beautiful, emotional story. You ready, Score Boy? Give this gurl a 10 from Miss Carlotta!"

Harloweena: "Child, everybody here knows I'm old school. And you went super old school tonight. I mean, I get it. You did something modern with old material. But it seemed just a little...slow. During the semi-finals, your act was super high energy. Here, in the finale, what happened? And I know you have a story to tell, and you got your point across beautifully, but I miss the energy from last time. I did love it, but I didn't love love it, you know what I mean? My score for you tonight is a 9."

Midge: "Let's talk mechanics here. Your use of costumes tonight is perfection. You moved from being an obedient, submissive handmaiden to being an unstoppable force of pure, prideful energy. Your lip-syncing is flawless. And I have to disagree with Harloweena, the energy at the end was explosive. And clearly personal to you. I did love love love it and I am proud to give you a score of 10."

King Janus: Twenty-nine for the Fabulous Fangula. Thank you, my dear."

Shouting to the crowd, "Are we ready? Are you ready? Let me hear some noi-oise!"

Janus pumps up the crowd, since this will be the final performance in this year's Drag Wars event. He wants it to be successful, since this was his idea, pitched to club management, to increase attendance and profits. For this first year, Janus had just selected the contestants on his own, but who knows what might spring from his creation during the next event?

"Here she comes, fresh off her perfect score last week. Let me hear you welcome the lady with the mega-watt personality, and the voice to match...here she is...Pridezilla!"

Channeling my inner Loretta Young, I make a grand entrance onto the stage. My look is one of campy sophistication, which is the oxymoronic way of stating that I look fucking fabulous.

My makeup, an homage to the hilarious Endora from *Bewitched*, is wildly colorful and splendidly outrageous. The music begins. This is all about camp, my dears, so I belt out "Let Me Entertain You" with the same gusto as Ethel Merman or Roz Russell. And, mimicking the choreography in *Gypsy,* I strut around the stage in a flashy red evening gown, with a faux fur stole around my shoulders, doing a striptease where I never actually strip at all. Call me Gypsy Pridezilla Lee!

I'm selling it and the audience is definitely buying it. Tips galore come my way.

As the first song ends, snippets of Agnes Moorehead, in the role of Endora, are played by the DJ. I go down into the audience, calling different guys there, "Derwood," "Darwin," "Dum-Dum," "Delwood," and "Delmore," all in the voice of the beloved Endora character. Of course, she refused to ever call Darren by his proper name on the TV show.

As I play this part, I'm twitching my nose, and while wearing a pair of cat's-eye glasses, I perform a little magic of my own, touching the sensors on the side of the frames, causing red lasers to shoot out from my eyes. Or so it appears, to the utter delight of the audience.

Returning to center stage, I perform a medley of some of the most dramatic songs ever performed, but my renditions are pure camp. Short snippets from Shirley Bassey singing "I Who Have Nothing," Peggy Lee crooning "Is That All There Is," and even Johnny Mathis performing "Misty," all done in homage to classic songs and voices. Everything I do on the stage is exaggerated to the 1000th degree.

I want to impress the judges with my dancing abilities, so I make my best moves during the Overture from "All That Jazz." This big gurl isn't shy, shimmying and shaking with the fast beat of the tune.

Then, the time for the final act arrives. The music goes silent for 10 seconds, as planned. I walk into the audience, pretending to search for someone, and then I see him. A beautiful, sleek, dark-skinned young man, wearing only very short, tight, white gym shorts, with a classic white Bike jockstrap underneath and white suspenders, perched at the bar, sipping a cocktail. That baby face paired with his athletic body, makes him a prize.

Though we act like this is a chance encounter, Divinity had suggested this college student from our neighborhood to me when I told her about my plans for the act.

I pull his arm, trying to bring him onto the stage. He resists at first, acting shy, but eventually, he allows me to lead him up for what will be my grand finale.

The music starts, and I begin the act, dancing sexily around him as I position him on all fours atop a table that Score Boy had rolled onto the stage while all eyes were on me.

The music, unfamiliar to most of the club-goers, has a strong beat and few lyrics—"Jungle Fever" by Chakachas. When the song gets to the part with the heavy breathing and sexy sighing, I pour it on thick, rubbing my hands all over the young man before me, lowering his suspenders and then eventually pulling down the back of his shorts, exposing his beautifully shaped Black buns for the audience.

Though he was told to remain still throughout the performance, he feels the beat of the song and begins thrusting, actually making the performance even better than I had expected.

During the song, he wriggles out of his shorts, wearing just his jock, and I know the audience enjoys the sight of that bulging package. *Yes, this is perfect*, I'm thinking, as I continue to massage his taut body.

Near the song's climax, I do just as Ruby's brother, in the role of Rubee Red Lips, did on stage many years before. Displaying my hand for all to see, I lick my middle finger and then slowly make it appear as if I'm penetrating the boy. No real penetration occurs, of course. It's an act, not a sexual encounter.

But the audience erupts at the sight, roaring with delight. I'm excited beyond words.

For the finale, as the song ends, I "withdraw" my finger, holding it high in the air and then sticking it into my mouth, sucking on it, while at the same time, smacking my young accomplice on his ass cheeks, dismissing him back into the crowd to have fun with his waiting friends.

With that, I take one final grand bow and blow kisses to my adoring fans.

Janus doesn't have time to say anything before Harloweena speaks.

"How in the name of holy hell did you ever know about that song and about that act? I know my bestie from many years ago, a grand Queen named Rubee Red Lips, is looking down on us right now and fucking laughing her ass off with delight. Oh my god, I wish Rubee could have been here to see this. Pridezilla, you have done us an honor tonight. The entire act was perfect, but you went so far over the top with that ending. A 10, 10, 10 from me!"

Carlotta: "Honestly, I don't even have words. From start to finish, this is perfection. And oh my darling, you do make one fabulous Endora. The nose twitch? Perfecto! The bit about the names of the husband on the show? Too fuckin' funny. And your act there at the end? Damn, gurl, you lit that stage on fire! A perfect 10 from me!"

Midge: "It always comes down to me, doesn't it? The little man with the big vote tonight. Just like it should be, right? Anyway, enough about me. This is your night, child. You came up with the perfect combination of glam, camp, comedy, and sexiness. This is how drag used to be. Fun and exciting, and campy as hell. I loved every bit of it. There can be no question, for the second week in a row, you deserve a perfect score of 10, with a perfect total of 30. Do your work, Score Boy!"

"We have a new Queen tonight," Janus shouts into his mike. "Make no mistake, the lady has earned it. Now, where is that Pink Tiara?"

Janus acts as if he's searching for the crown, as Score Boy pretends to hide it behind his back. The DJ is playing "Dancing Queen" by ABBA, but at a lower volume than usual.

"Any words for your fans out there?" King Janus asks me.

"First, thank you. This means a lot to me. You'll never really know, but let me say that I do appreciate you and thank you for your support. Now come on, ain't it time for me to get crowned?"

"Yes, it is," Janus laughs.

"Midge, will you do the honors, please?"

Midge jumps off her chair, grabs the Pink Tiara from Score Boy, and prances over to center stage.

"By the power vested to me by the good people of Oz...oh no, sorry, that's a different scene," Midge says, bringing screams of laughter from all, but especially the Snark Sharks, who always enjoy a good *Wizard of Oz* reference.

I bend down to accept the crown, but Midge has other ideas. "No, your Majesty, your highness, your Pridezilliness, please allow me. A little help here, Janus, if you're not too busy staring at that cute Score Boy. Or maybe the *Jungle Fever* boy caught your eye?"

Janus lifts up Midge, holding her high, and Midge places the coveted Pink Tiara on my Endora wig. I bow graciously to my "subjects" in the audience.

"And don't forget this, your prize money—a cool two thousand in cash. Now let me know if you need any bodyguards to protect you from those thieves out there," he jokes.

"And with that, the Drag Wars 2024 is now complete. This is your King Janus, saying thank you and we hope to see you for a new competition sometime soon. Good night, everybody, and don't forget to tip your bartenders tonight!"

Backstage, I'm met by Bobby and Ruby, who had permission from Janus to watch my act from the side of the stage and to come back here to celebrate with me. I'm sorry to see that Fangula has already left the area, though I find a single yellow rose on my dressing table. The note beside it reads:

"Loved your performance. You deserved to win.

Best,

Fangula"

Bobby and I are ready to celebrate. I don't need or want a big party, nothing like that. I don't feel the need to immediately announce my win on social media, hoping for a frenzy of attention. A quiet celebration suits me just fine. Social media can wait until tomorrow, at least.

We drive Ruby home and head for Bobby's place. Our celebration is the best kind. Personal and intimate. First, I fuck him. Then, he fucks me.

Did I wear my pink tiara the entire time? Damn straight, I did. After all...

I'm the motherfucking Queen of Drag Wars!

THE COMEBACK

F our days later, I'm still crying in my room, all alone and feeling so very lonely. After losing to Pridezilla, my IG was flooded with comments. Many of them were positive messages of support. But others were ugly, calling me a loser, lacking talent, criticizing every aspect of the show.

I want to be strong. Honestly, if I plan to survive in this world, I have to be stronger than this. I don't want to be a snowflake, melting at the first sign of criticism. But this loss hurt me. I hope it won't be long before my confidence returns.

I had big plans for celebrating my win. First, it was important for me to cause a social media frenzy, with announcements on all the major platforms, including posting videos of the moment the pink tiara was placed upon my beautiful self. Then, a night of partying, with an actual entourage of fans who would spend the night adoring me, telling me all about my fabulosity.

And I still want a horde of fans. I still want an entourage. Maybe I just have to start smaller. Oh, and I've decided what I want to call my fans. Not the Littles and not the Cruzers. Not even the Vamps. I'm going to call my babies the Fangulettes.

Of course, I still haven't forgotten about merchandising. I already had merch created for my store, with my photo and the words "Winner of Drag Wars 2024" splashed everywhere. Now, all that work had been wasted. My disappointment is a bad taste that I can't quite swallow away.

Music is my salvation. I first turn to my Latina sheroes, streaming beautiful songs by Kany Garcia, Karol G, Becky G, Natti Natasha and others. Sometimes, I don't understand every word of the Spanish lyrics, but that doesn't keep me from inhaling the strength and power of these artists for myself. I don't limit myself to the female artists, though they speak to me more directly.

The men, including Maluma, Bad Bunny, Romeo Santos and, of course, Ozuna, eventually lift me out of my state of morose indifference.

I wonder if these and other artists truly understand the power they have to transform and heal the lives of people like me, in deep pain, but wanting to overcome that and find my own successes in life.

Luisito came over to visit, just for sex. His only interest is in my bussy. When it comes to emotional support, he's a zero. I gotta get rid of that loser sometime soon, but for right now, the sex takes my mind off of the pain.

The isolation and fear are suffocating me, drowning me in a sea of intolerance, ignorance and hatred. These days have shown me that this struggle is too much for me to handle alone. I need to reach out, but it feels like I've been abandoned.

My energy has been drained. I'm so fatigued, I feel my body melting into the furniture. This isn't like me at all. I need to take steps to snap out of it.

How is it that my life went so quickly from one where I was busy taking care of the needs of others, to this point, where it feels like no one even knows that I exist?

Before I reach out to anyone, I have to find a way to bring some sense of inner peace to my being. I remember playing dress up with Slash, before...before...well, I don't want to think about that. But we'd play games, including getting dressed up in Mami's clothes. I'd act glamorous, holding a mirror in front of me and affirming. "Mirror, mirror in my hand. Could I be any more grand?"

I grab my mirror from the dresser and practice. After three or four times, I begin to believe it. I have to be grand. I have a need to be a performer. I want to be a Drag Queen Extraordinaire. I can come back from this defeat. This is not the end for Fangula.

Ready to take that first, baby step forward, I send a text to Divinity.

"Gurl, can we talk? I need a friend right now. I need a sister."

Two hours later, both Divinity and Pridezilla are walking towards my door.

"Gurl, you gotta get yourself together. And you really gotta get yourself outta this place."

Divinity is reacting to the mess in the house. I've been too depressed to take care of anything mundane, like washing dishes or mopping floors.

"And where exactly would I be going?"

Pridezilla speaks up. "We're starting a house—a house of Queens. Divinity is Mother Superior. I'm one of the gurls. Whaddya think? Care to join us? Be one of the gurls?"

It takes me all of 10 seconds to think about it. With Mami gone, Carlito/Cobra/Cookie gone, with Slash gone, Mateo gone, well, what's holding me here? Nothing. Plus, it's just a move to West Philly, not across the world. And if it doesn't work out, well, they never said it had to be permanent. So why not give it a try?

"Yes, I'd love to be one of the gurls, one of your gurls, Mother Divinity."

Except for Friday nights at the club, I've never felt like I had a place where I truly belonged. I want a home. I want a family. Maybe this is what I'm looking for. There's only one way to find out.

"Let's go, ladies!"

Let's Be Legend.

The End

Also by

Robert A. Karl

The CLUBBED Trilogy
CLUBBED: A Story of Gay Love: Trials, Tribulations and Triumphs
CLUBBED TWO: Anxiety, Anger, Activism
CLUBBED THREE: Darkness and Light
The Goldies: 50th High School Reunion
If you enjoyed DRAG WARS: Fangula vs Pridezilla,
please leave a rating/review on Amazon and Goodreads.

About the author

Robert A. Karl is a native son of Philadelphia, PA, a retired educator, a queer author and an advocate for the LGBTQ+ community. He now resides in San Juan, Puerto Rico, where he enjoys the beauty and culture of La Isla del Encanto, the Island of Enchantment.

Visit the author's website at: robertkarlauthor.com

Visit the author's online shop at: clubpride.org

Visit Fangula's website at: fangula.com

Contact the author at: robert.karl.author@gmail.com